About the Author

Leon Reid has been a member of Romance Writers of America RWA, has twenty years of experience in public speaking, and has thirty years of experience of writing short stories, and articles. The author achieved a Doctor of Strategic Leadership from Liberty University. He currently works as a senior specialist. He is married with three daughters.

Infatuation

Leon Reid

Infatuation

Olympia Publishers
London

www.olympiapublishers.com
OLYMPIA PAPERBACK EDITION

Copyright © Leon Reid 2024

The right of Leon Reid to be identified as author of
this work has been asserted in accordance with sections 77 and 78 of
the Copyright, Designs and Patents Act 1988.

All Rights Reserved

No reproduction, copy or transmission of this publication
may be made without written permission.
No paragraph of this publication may be reproduced,
copied or transmitted save with the written permission of the publisher,
or in accordance with the provisions
of the Copyright Act 1956 (as amended).

Any person who commits any unauthorised act in relation to
this publication may be liable to criminal
prosecution and civil claims for damage.

A CIP catalogue record for this title is
available from the British Library.

ISBN: 978-1-80439-561-5

This is a work of fiction.
Names, characters, places and incidents originate from the writer's
imagination. Any resemblance to actual persons, living or dead, is
purely coincidental.

First Published in 2024

Olympia Publishers
Tallis House
2 Tallis Street
London
EC4Y 0AB

Printed in Great Britain

Dedication

I would like to dedicate this book to my wife, Marlene, and all the ladies who are searching for love.

Acknowledgments

I want to acknowledge my wife, Marlene, who breathe life into these stories, my daughter, Makayla, who helped to make the book relatable to real-life situations, and to my friends who encourage me to finish this book.

CHAPTER 1

I have an idea. Experiencing infatuation feels like love. Parsing emotions are complex and provide little comfort to a delicate soul. As the visuals of our eyes transcend messages to our hearts, we imagine happiness from perfect conversations. I've spent several hours comparing love and infatuation, and my observations are revealing.

Infatuation is a foolish passion or unreasonable attraction that we feel toward each other. We gravitate to the person that our imagination convinces us to be our perfect soulmate. Our hearts pound heavily thinking about fairytales and exaggerating every personal contact that we encounter. Our appetite for love is real. Understanding the difference is a challenge. Can we control our adrenaline as rational beings? The straddle of loneliness is a feature of our existence.

This is strange. Love and infatuation are the stars of the same book. They play the same role in every movie. But one tends to hurt more. Why do my heart and my ego tend to conflict? As a scholar of love, I should know.

It's the summer of relationships. The clock just strikes three p.m. and I have a few hours left at the garage. With several cars to finish, I was trapped with other employees. It is like solitary confinement where we were stacked, fighting the feeling of tiredness and the vehicle oil all over our uniforms. The time will not go by. I watched the clock every minute and I was convinced that the time was paused. We engage in friendly banter, mocking each other on relationships and social issues. I hate gestures, but it's a technique that keeps us sane.

For anyone who does not know me, here is some information: I am Dan Walker. I'm the senior mechanic at Emotions Automotive. It is a large automotive business located in Charlotte, North Carolina. After completing an associate degree in auto mechanics, I enrolled at the University of North Carolina at Charlotte, pursuing a degree in mechanical engineering.

It was almost five p.m. and my name echoed across the floor from pit ten. Blasting in the work area was like loudspeakers at the airport.

"Here I am. What do you want? Why are you shouting my name, Brandon?" A burst of loud laughter erupts from the floor. All the coworkers knew that it was time for matchmaking.

"I want to remind you that we are going to my cousin's birthday party tonight," replied Brandon. "I will not take no for an answer."

Brandon is my best friend. Ever since I broke up with my high school girlfriend of seven years, Brandon took on the role of counselor. His objective is to find my true love. Even though it was a role that he assumed, I played along with his charade. The gravity of the separation almost leads me to depression. For a seven-year dream came crashing down in one day. The transition was hard, but my friends stood by me. On the outside, I show strength, but on the inside, I was broken. When I was alone, I became afraid. Crumbled to the world, I pray that it was a dream every night I went to bed. It was fascinating how loneliness played with my emotions. Transforming midnight shadows into my high school crush. How come the window which was the prime attraction in my house, became a weapon to my mind? The reality of relationships proves harder than I think.

"What time is the party?"

There was a short pause as if he was expecting me to say no. Maybe I was weary from the day's work. The silence was telling. It was obvious that my coworkers were listening to the conversation. I could hear their hearts beating, waiting for the answers.

Finally, "Nine p.m." Brandon blurted.

There were whispers. Maybe they were surprised by my answer. The shadow of loneliness was still haunting me. Parading in my ex-girlfriend's statue, symbolizing the human companionship that I missed. Intimate moments we had continued to play in my mind. Her soft-spoken words whispered in my ears, and the embrace that would last forever. My coworkers expected me to decline the invitation and recoil to self-pity. Maybe it is time to explore what the world has to offer.

"I will meet you there at nine p.m. sharp," I shouted to my wider audience.

"Mmm" was the loud gasp from the room as if my coworkers rehearse the line. "What is the dress code, Brandon?"

He answered in a jeering but enthusiastic tone, "Semi-formal, a nice pair of jeans and your best blazer."

"Got it, I will try my best."

My coworkers were cheering. Was it out of pity or support? They remembered the days when I was full of life. Glaring to the sound of soul and R&B music. Nothing would bother me. I was happy. I would coach employees about relationships. Now, I am grumpy. I complain about everything. Simple gestures from people annoy me. Suddenly there was a loud shout from Jen, the only female mechanic at the company.

"You go player, I know you still got it"

"Thank you, Jen," I responded, "I hope I still do," to the sound of loud laughter. This might be the boost I needed. Approval from a female will boost my effort. Her complement turns the hands in my clock. It starts ticking again. The wounds of darkness appear a little brighter. It was like a love angel appeared before me and convinced me that the world has a lot to offer.

On my way from work, this time was different. My mind was open to dating again. The inner and outer beauty of women were appearing again. I was smiling inside. It was a moment. The acceptance that my previous relationship was over, and it was time to move on. My greatest victory was the realization that dating was out of practicality. It either works or it doesn't. It hardens the minds of lonely people open to dating and it comes with headaches, heartache, heartbreak, disappointments, and happiness.

The party was all about fun. I went there with an open mind. The hope of meeting people. Anything can happen. I was ready to explore all sundries. Brandon introduces me to all his friends and acquaintances. I met many female companions. We talk, laugh, and dance. It was a joyous occasion. However, there was no connection. That is OK. It was the start of a process. The start of a long journey. The journey to find my soulmate. Love should not have a standard, but the connection should be obvious. I am not tempted to use my previous relationship as a milepost, but the feeling and camaraderie can be used as a guide in the process.

It is not my view that God chooses a person for me to love. But through socialization, true love can be achieved. The rose may not fall from heaven, but blooms in perfect formation from my back garden. It is the color of love that matches this flower on the day of harvest. My patience helps me to develop perfect conversations. Beauty is in the eyes of the beholder, and once I am searching for it, I will find it.

At four in the morning, I beckoned Brandon that it was my time to go. In a funny gest, he said. "You are leaving already? The party is just starting."

"Yea, it's past bedtime," I suggested.

"I am glad that you enjoyed yourself, we should do this again sometime."

"Anytime you are ready, Brandon, just let me know."

Reality can be my worst enemy. Arriving home in the wee of the morning, the birds are about to start their daily shores, chirping in excitement for my effort with other insects joining. The darkness was evident. Trying to force me into remission. The lonely house welcomes me home. Reminding me that something was missing. Forcing me to explain that I am working on it. This time was different. Rather than lying in the cloak of darkness reminiscing about my previous relationship, and basking in sadness, I picture a great woman that I will meet in the future. It was a breath of fresh air. I command the moment and invigorate positive energy.

I quickly fell asleep. A change from my nightly toss and turn trying to sleep. I had a dream. Departing from the nightmares of my past. It was a quiet night. We were having dinner on the back porch. The smell of baby back rib spread across the house. A combination of green bean, macaroni, and cheese complemented by my best bottle of red wine. This was the first time that I cooked for her. With six candles lighting up the night sky, her red dress creates a backdrop for the evening, moving in unison with the trees and her perfume invigorates the atmosphere. Her eyes form a bond of light from my wine glass. The brightest light I have ever seen. Not a light to damage the eyes, but to form a sensation that life is worth living.

After hours of conversation, she fell asleep in my arms. It was the first time I slept outside. I did not want to disturb the moment. God was also sanctioning the evening. It was the closest the stars had ever been. They were in a formation. It appears to be in the form of a heart, at times, two hearts, and at another time both hearts join to form one. The union in the sky might be a message that love is in the air. Whatever it was, it felt good.

I was awoken by the sun shining through the window. It was almost midday. Wow. Did I sleep for almost ten hours? Feeling refreshed as if I was just coming from the beach. I glanced across the bed and there was no one there. It was all a dream. What was her name? It did not matter because it was beautiful. The lady in red symbolizes the beginning of my journey. A journey in search of love. I still picture her beautiful eyes reflecting from the wine glass.

Suddenly, the doorbell rang. Who could it be? I rushed to the door hoping that it was the lady in the red dress.

"How are you?" my mother shouted as she forced herself inside the house.

"I have been calling you all morning and you are not answering."

"I was asleep, Mom."

"Asleep?" she replied. "You never sleep."

Mom was feeling my neck to see if I had a fever. She thought I was sick or dying. The bag in her hands contains breakfast from IHOP. My mom checks on me every weekend. If I don't go over to her house, she will find herself at mine. I told her that I want to give the house a spring cleaning. She was surprised but happy.

"Who is she, and when can I meet her? What is her name?" and the questions keep coming. I wanted to say it was the lady in the red dress, but I didn't know her name. I smiled and kissed her on the cheek.

"Come on, I am waiting," she pressed.

"No one yet, Mom, but I am ready to start dating again."

I could see the joy in her eyes as she hugged me tighter. For she knew that she had her son back. The cleaning company arrived, and the house was spotless. Mom chided me to keep it that way and promised to punish me if I didn't.

CHAPTER 2

Waking up by myself is not a choice, but a lifestyle forced on me through the process of infatuation. But I am seeing the light. Months of socialization help me to understand the mechanics of dating. It is easier with my support team, my mom, my best friend, and coworkers. After a hard day's work and no school assignment, I opt to take a bath. The hope is to curl up in the coach and watch a movie. In the shower, the water was punishing me. The droplets from the faucet were larger than normal. It had a crystal look with heat that could cook a three-course meal. The more I adjust, the harsher it gets. I wonder in my mind, what did I do? The shower kept me in suspense. My body was bruised from the assault.

    I was scrolling to find a good movie when the phone rang. The number was familiar. My heart started beating very fast. What should I do? She had not called me in two years. I was confused. I got a bottle of water from the kitchen. One sip and it was finished. The phone still rings. It appears to be getting louder. So loud that it was giving me a headache. At one point, it sounds like the bell that rings at my church on a Sunday. In my mind, I want it to stop, but my heart wants Kylee's name permanently on the screen.

    The shower was trying to tell me something earlier. Should I take a second bath to understand the message? I was nervous. After five rings, the phone stopped. I was staring at the screen. I wanted to call her back, but I was afraid that the shower would punish me for any mistake. Kylee had moved to live in New York after starting her modeling career. Immediately after accepting the job, she informed me that it was over. Not just over, she was dating. She refuses to take any of my calls and at one point blocks by number.

Thank God it was over, but before I could parse my thoughts, the phone start ringing again. I was experiencing confusion with confidence. Confidence because I was communicating with people regularly and understanding the dynamics of dating. Confusion because I did not know what to do. She was my first love, the woman who broke my heart. What does she want? I decided to find out.

I picked up the phone. My hands were trembling. It appears that I was losing my sight as everything in the house was blurred. My tongue feels heavy. Am I having a stroke?

"Hi, Dan, this is Kylee."

It was like an angel whispering. I couldn't hear anything. Maybe I am reading too much into this call. I slap myself in the face to bring myself back to reality.

"Dan, are you there?" she echoed.

"H-h-h-hi, h-h-h-I." This is the first time I discovered I had a stutter. The words would not come out. I used to talk to Kylee for several hours per day for seven years. I freeze.

"It's me silly, did the cat get your tongue?"

All I could hear were several selections of James Ingram's songs. As I mustered the courage to gather my thoughts, it was clear that I was still in love with her. It affected my emotional state and might affect my judgment. After five minutes my silence was broken.

"How are you?"

"Could be better," she replied. "I am back in town and was

wondering if you want to get a drink."

"Sure, Kylee, let me know the time and place."

"Charlotte Luxury Lounge, eight p.m. sharp."

"I will see you there."

As I hung up, I wondered what was happening. Is Kylee coming back into my life? I did not want to know the answer. The bitterness that was on the tip of my tongue got sweeter. There was a calm in the house. It was like all the furniture in the house started to whisper. I could not decipher what they were saying but I did not care.

I rushed to the store to get a new suit. The balance in my account was low. It was not enough to pay my monthly expenses, but I did not care. All I could think about was the love of my life. I must look my best. The suit was expensive, but the occasion meets the moment.

"What's the occasion?" the store attendant asked.

"I am reuniting with the love of my life," as the glee on my face was obvious.

"You must love her. You are not interested in the price of the suit. My job is to ensure that you get the best."

As the attendant selected my attire, she was pleased. I tried it on, it fit perfectly. It was like a wedding, and I was the perfect groom. Mimicking the appearance of the store mannequin, I was ready to meet my queen. The fabric perfectly aligns with my physique, providing a cover that is easy to attract. Almost like flirting, the store attendant admires the fashion. This was a perfect work of art. She clutched her hands around mine like a bride holding her husband. The gentle way she treats the fabric was reminiscent of her passion for fashion. Massaging the seams to create a buffer between my body and the jacket.

"You look handsome. The lady will be happy to be by your

side."

"Thank you, madam, for your kind words," as I watched her place my purchase in a bag. She wished me well and encouraged me to visit again.

Eager for the moment, I left my house early. The hope was to have a thirty-minute head start. Attired in a pair of black pants, a sky-blue shirt, and a black jacket, I placed myself in line for the crown. The tailored stitched suit provides a sense of self-assurance that any man craves for. The Fendi cologne invigorates an extra buffer. I was like a mobile flower garden, fermenting the air with every step I made.

My car was cleaned with a new air freshener. The rose-scented fragrance uplifts the mood of the moment and protects my delicate innocence. As the obedience of the car beckons to people along the way, it appears that she was creating a salvatory moment. I can't remember passing any of the major milestones as my mind was occupied. Combing all the possibilities of life to end this night with a happy ending. Striving to return to the days when love was strong.

The present I bought was from her favorite jewelry store. A hand-engraved chain linked fourteen karat gold with a half-inch diamond heart-shaped pendant. The chain represents a rope that will bind our love forever, and the diamond heart echoes my devoted love. It is a symbol of my heart given to the lady who I want to spend the rest of my life with. It should remind her of the great moments that we had. To complement the occasion, I ordered fifteen red roses. I reserved a table for two next to the window. I ordered the best bottle of red wine and tipped the waiter to play Kylee's favorite James Ingram song, "Just Once." Seven candles were placed on the table, each representing the years that we were together. With an eighth candle representing the future. Once the mood was right, Kylee would light it to confirm continuity.

The table is obvious to every patron. I was the center of attention, and they were waiting to meet the lucky lady. The celebrity moment feels good. I was like a famous singer about to perform at a concert. The fans are cheering, waiting for me to appear on stage. The evening started with thirty minutes of fireworks. Everybody is waiting for the MC to make the announcement.

There was a large clock in the dining room. Reminding me every minute of the evening. Cheer me for a job well done. Before I knew it, it was nine p.m. and Kylee was late. The clock was getting louder. However, it didn't matter, as it was worth the wait. By ten p.m., I was concerned. The clock became unbearable. It was mocking me. The hands were beating four to six times per second.

The patrons at the restaurant started to show their sympathies. It was the most humiliating day of my life. It appears that I lost my sight. I was losing my mind. This was unbelievable. The darkness in the room was evident. People were consoling me. It felt like a funeral. Someone close to me had passed. I could not cry. Kylee was a no-show. At one point, I pinched myself. I was hoping that I was dreaming and wanted to wake up. As the sound from James Ingram echoes in my head, I wonder what I did wrong.

The restaurant was understandable. Who wouldn't? Out of pity, they were trying to salvage what they could. I wanted to cry but there were no tears. I could feel the sun beaming on my face in the middle of the night. Finding time to drown out the moon and stars. People are trying to convince me that it was her loss. How could that be? I spent all my savings on the evening. They are just trying to comfort me.

Several patrons offered to buy me a drink, but I want to remain sober. I did not have an appetite anyway. The shower in my house was trying to tell me something. Love can be brutal sometimes. My expectations were too high. I have developed a phobia of reality in the last two months. It was the truth. The reality is that life is not a quick fix. I need to live every moment like it was yesterday.

With a dark cloud over my head, I thanked everyone and left. I must face the empty house. Salvage my bride and move on. In my bed, I struggle to understand what happened. Was it the work of God, or the love monster trying to defeat me? Whatever it was, it would not break my spirit. That night I prayed a special prayer and then fell asleep. The best part of the night was that the lady in red was in my dream.

The next day I reached out to Kylee. Not to set up another date, but to have closure. It was a surreal moment. To learn that she did not even remember our date. Kylee also had problems of her own. She lost her modeling job and broke up with her boyfriend. The courtesy call to her was just to see if I was still interested in her.

At first, I was mad. How could someone be so selfish? But I realize that she would have used me until she finds the next opportunity. After a long discussion, I agree that she could meet me at my house to continue talking. I had no expectations. My mind was conditioned to move on. I was meeting Kylee out of courtesy. I will never forgive her for the embarrassment that she causes me.

Suddenly, an Uber drove up. It was Kylee. She did not have a car as the dealership repossessed it. I was shocked. Kylee looked different. The loss of her modeling job affected her life.

She was depressed and placed on medication. She hugged me. I didn't know if I should hug her back.

"Did you miss me, Dan?" she shouted. She looks pale as if she had not seen the sun for months. Kylee pretends as if last night didn't happen.

"I am better, long time no see," as I stared at her in disbelief.

"You like what you see?" she laughs out loud.

"You look all right…"

I could not tell her the truth. It appears that the love of my life had been tortured enough. The bags under her eyes were elevated. It appears that Kylee had not slept in months. Maybe Karma is against her for her misdeeds, but who am I to judge? My job is to assist her the best I can to help her through this difficult time.

CHAPTER 3

The shrapnel of a bad relationship was evident in Kylee, and I feel that I am obligated to help her get over it. A broken heart is like a vacuum cleaner, sucking the life out of its victims. I should know. I feel that pain every day. Love can make people do crazy things. I am prepared to help the person who inflicts the greatest pain on me. In a normal world, I would be celebrating her demise. But I feel guilty. Maybe I was responsible. If I was there for her, she would still be perfect. Kylee would not have the urge to cheat on me.

After several sessions with the doctor and medications, there were improvements in Kylee's physical appearance. The glee starts to appear in her eyes again. The precious flower begins to emerge from the dust. The resurrection of Christ was a motivating force. Her clothing started to take shape again. The stars were appearing in the night skies. I was determined to erase from my memory the betrayal, but it was easier said than done. Was Kylee the lady in the red dress from my dream? Time will tell.

It was a Sunday. I was preparing dinner. Kylee asks to come by my house, and I agree. It was not a date, but my effort needs to be special. The odds of creating a romantic climate were remote. I was not ready to experience that emotional trauma again. My effort was basic but curious. I asked her to wear her favorite red dress. It was a social experiment. I wanted to see if any sexual tension would spark. Emerging from a romantic drought would rekindle a lifetime of love in my life. I reminded myself to tamper with expectations.

The doorbell rings. Kylee was at the door. Like a motion picture, she emerges from the shadows. Representing an attractive woman but not stealing the moment. It appears that the drumbeat was too long. The introduction was exaggerated. The scheme was still dark. I was waiting for someone to turn on the light. I flipped the light switch, but it did not make a difference. Maybe it was all in my head. Let me be patient.

"Are you going to greet me with a kiss?" she demanded.

"Sure."

I stared in disbelief as she embraced me with her tiny hands. Her lips connect with mine for the first time in two years. I was expecting to hear fireworks in my head. It was supposed to be my 4th of July moment. No one paid the organizers, and the show was canceled. The kiss lasted for almost one minute. It was ordinary. For a moment, I thought it did not happen.

"It is time to eat, and I am starving."

"I guess we have the whole night," she suggested.

"We will see, Kylee."

I stared at her dress. Expecting to be moved. I was disappointed. Maybe I was used to being with a supermodel with perfect shape. Maybe I was still upset with her. I try to find every rationale for my actions. It was not there.

"Why are you staring, you want to own my dress?"

I smiled and indicated that it was time to eat. Everything was different. The emotions and sexual tension that was burning for this lady were dissipating. It was demoted to a mission to help Kylee overcome her depression. However, Kylee had other ideas.

"Dan, can we watch a movie? I have one in my bag."

"Sure."

As I placed the movie in the player, Kylee sat closer to me. Her arm was extended toward my chest, moving her head momentarily and placing it on my left shoulder, and rubbing her hair against my neck while massaging my knees. As she was about to kiss me, I indicated that I was going to clean up the kitchen. This was an excuse to get out of this situation. I was nervous.

I spent almost two hours in the kitchen washing two dishes. The whole time I was reminiscing on the years we had been together. I was in a dark place. I was not prepared to throw away all the efforts of my mother and friends. Kylee wanted us to start dating again because of her depression. She was the victim and was using me for the rebound.

I decided that we were going to have a real discussion. It was an honest conversation about being her friend. At this point, I will follow my heart. My heart is not interested in an intimate relationship with Kylee right now. As I stepped into the living room, I noticed Kylee was asleep. Lying on the couch in silk lingerie exposing herself to the element. Her body was positioned to indicate her intent.

Should I wake her up and tell her it was time for her to go? Where is my humanity? I reach for the blanket and cover her, and adjust the thermostat so the temperature would be manageable. I turn the light off and ascend to my room. I could hear the furniture complimenting me for my kindness. Love should extract the best in all humans, not take advantage of a human in her vulnerabilities.

I went to bed with a clear conscience. Knowing fully that my masculinity causes me to feel some urges. However, my heart got the better of me. The passion for civility drowns out the feeling of infatuation. It allows me to reclaim my manhood with pride. I am conscious of the future ahead and determined once again to find true love. The love and approval I once thirsted for in Kylee dissipated. The naked angel of love was a magnet to my sexual craven. I have lost my appetite.

The next morning, I woke up early. I was almost finished preparing breakfast when Kylee sneaks up and hugs me from behind. I could feel her birthday suit pressed against my body, caressing my chest, electrifying some fuse in my body. But it was not enough to start the engine. Advancing the gains of her hands leaves me numb. I was visibly shaking. Should I play along and see where it leads? By that time, my eyes were closed. I was losing consciousness. I was about to cave when I smelled the eggs burning.

Her grip was tight but gentle. She was devouring her predator without saying a word. I released her hands and turned off the stove. I barely found the energy to move my legs. I regained self-consciousness. The kitchen was still dark. Dark from the seduction attempts. Her small but savage hands were almost deadly. I could see her smile. Kylee knew the impact that her actions were having on me. For the sake of love, I must resist.

"It's time to eat Kylee, please join me," as I wobble to the small table in the kitchen.

"Sure, baby, can you pass my dress for me."

"With all pleasure. What are your plans for today?"

"I am going to the hairdresser, unless you want me to stay here with you?"

"That would be nice, but I am going to run some errands for my mom shortly. Maybe some other time."

"That's a deal," Kylee replied.

With a curious look on her face, we had breakfast. This illuminates several discussions and the necessity for us to remain close friends. Any suggestions of a social relationship were useless as Kylee believes that whatever she says goes. At this point, I realize why she treats me this way. Kylee thought I was a supplicant to her desire. She could have and reject me whenever she wants. I was the substitute teacher in her school.

To Her Majesty, I was a peasant. A victim of love that was captured for seven years. Blinded by the darkness of my self-preservation. It was difficult to parse love from infatuation. But I realized that it was time to grow up. Not in the physical sense, but to mature in relationships. To master the dynamics of relationships. Determine to find a union where both parties find happiness on mutual terms. Where the definition of love is not semantic.

"Can I see you later, Dan?"

"Maybe, I will see how it goes. I have a lot to do today but once I am finished, I will let you know." With a nod of the head in approval, Kylee left. I have a mission for the day. The mission is to find enough things to do that will keep me up until tomorrow when it is time to go to work. I spent about four hours at the library doing some research on automation in auto mechanics. The project is due in two weeks, but I have the time.

In the evening, I went to my mom's house for dinner. As usual, she was asking me about my love life. Although she was nosy, she was also concerned. I could not tell her about Kylee. Not that she slept over last night or that she stood me up at the restaurant. My mother knew how she treated me and the difficulty I had getting over the breakup. It was like my mom was a clairvoyant. At dinner, she asks me when was the last time seen or spoke with Kylee.

"Who?" I pretend not to know who she was talking to or hear what she says.

"Why are you acting so guilty, my son?"

"Me, no, oh, Kylee?"

"Boy, are you getting crazy. Look how you react just hearing that girl's name. I can tell that you are still hurt. God will send a good woman for you."

"I believe you, Mom." I omit to tell my mother anything that happened with Kylee.

"I heard that she is back in town and nature was not good to her. My God is not sleeping."

From listening to my mom, I could tell that she does not want Kylee one hundred miles near me. Kylee was calling me, but I did not answer. She texted me to find out what time I was going to be finished. I indicated that I was not leaving my mom's house before nine. I already decided that I was not going to see her that night, but I was letting the day play out. As strong as I believe I was, I am still human. The synergy of life can be rebuffed if we prevent things from happening. I might not be as strong as the last time.

Kylee called and texted a couple more times until she realized that it was not going to happen. Relationships are a strange phenomenon and if I do not take control of my destiny, then someone will take control of me. The milk of loneliness will curdle in my sight. For the thrust of survival in a savvy world where love predators are waiting to pounce cannot be allowed to run loose. I have a dream and that dream is to find true love. I believe that can only happen when I identify that lady in the red dress. I was convinced that Kylee is not that woman. I might want perfection, but that is not the point. Whatever form of love appears, I am ready to embrace it.

CHAPTER 4

After an eventful weekend, I went to work refreshed. I was determined to clear the backlog in the garage. Tom was my boss and quickly realized a change in my work attitude. Afraid to break the momentum, he remains quiet until lunch. By then, almost a hundred vehicles had passed through the service line.

"Are you working for my job?" Tom joked.

"No sir, I am just in a good mood."

"In the way you are going, we might not have anything to do tomorrow."

"I promise that I will leave some for the rest of the week, Tom."

"Keep up the good work."

I was motivated by the elements of life. The weekend creates a buffer in my life to strive for greater things. Refocusing my priorities on the things that matter most. Brandon was lurking in the wind. He was expecting me to share the good news with him. I couldn't, but I assured him that everything was fine. The hallmark of surprise was showing on my face. Why am I so happy? My theory was confirmed that I was finally over Kylee. Kylee was not prepared to accept rejection. It was as if she was stalking me. She texts me every hour of the day. If I did not respond to her text, she would call. I am cognizant of her mental and emotional state and was not willing to do anything to affect her health. However, I was not prepared to lead her on. My happiness is paramount. At some point, Kylee will realize that I moved on. Will she take my kindness for weakness? I hope not.

After work, I went to meet Tyler. Tyler is in my study group. We want to brainstorm some topics that the professor will teach next week. I was surprised that Tyler had company. He took his girlfriend with him. Lia was all over Tyler. The wheel of love is turning. I have never seen this before. Was this a model relationship? They were like a unit. One would start a sentence and the other would finish it. Once the sentence was finished, they would kiss in agreement.

I will introduce myself to Lia. Tyler would not allow me to have a conversation with her. My mind was straying. Was Lia a rare quality, or did she have a sister? It was difficult to find out as they were all over each other. The study was compromised, but the moment was beautiful. If Tyler would get one dollar every time he kisses Lia, he would be a rich man today. It is a couple that is overdoing it, but that extra action represents a type of love that should be cherished.

"Where did you guys meet?" I was curious. I was interested in following the same path to see if the results would be the same.

"We met on a dating site, Emotions Dating," they sing the answer like a chorus.

"You should check it out. Some nice people are there," explained Lia.

"I came across the profile for this catfish several months ago. I realized that we have a common interest and decided to contact him."

Lia is originally from Georgia. They have been together for over a year. The chemistry that they display is phenomenal. People think that love is blind; I beg to disagree. Their love is in its purest form and can be touched, felt, and embraced. I could feel a difference in the atmosphere whenever I was around them.

"We have great plans. In the fall, we intend to get married. Once we buy our home, we will start a family."

"A son," Tyler shouted.

"Or a daughter," Lia laughs out loud.

I was dumbfounded. My feelings have changed. There were cold bumps all over my body. For the first time, I was jealous of someone. Jealous not in a bad way. But wanting to be in a similar position. Longing to smell the air of love and to breathe life into my thoughts. I would stare at Lia and Tyler for long periods. Not in a creepy way, but to admire God's creation. I was convinced that the foundation of happiness can be developed through effective human interactions. I am a fallible being, but one who believes that perfection can be achieved by molding a relationship.

The camaraderie of Tyler and Lia is not just impacting me, but it was evident that other people in the café were enjoying their presence.

"Tyler, remember that you are here to study with Dan, my daughter's father needs to be an engineer."

"Or son," as they joked with each other.

"Out of curiosity, I realize that you want a daughter and Tyler wanted a son. What if you get the opposite of what you want?"

There was a pause. In my mind, I thought there was a disagreement in the relationship. Maybe they are not perfect after all. They looked at each other and smiled. I was taking notes. This is a learning experience. To understand love is to understand how couples maneuver their differences to achieve a comprise.

"We do not mind what type of baby we have. We joked out of curiosity because men tend to talk about sons and women talked about daughters. We think it is just a symbolic icebreaker."

I was surprised by the answers from Tyler and Lia nodded

her head in agreement. I am declaring this relationship perfect. As I grovel in my mind, I wonder if this should be a model relationship. Is this too perfect for me? Can the sanctity of love be rewritten in my mind? If hate has a space in their hearts, it could not breathe. Smoldered by the beauty of human emotions and entrenched in their subconsciousness. Who could imagine that people could fall in love so deeply?

There was not much that we could study as we were all distracted. Who wouldn't be? Seeing Tyler and Lia drinking one smoothie with two straws. Gobbling up the beverage in a coordinated effort while I fought to devour my soda, the feeling of loneliness was lingering in my mind. Lia returned to a seat in the corner to allow us to brainstorm some topics. I noticed that she was reading a book. It was a memoir from author Ingrid Green entitled *I Can't let this Kill Me*. The book explains her tumultuous marriage and struggles with depression. I decided to recommend the book to Kylee.

We spent the next two hours discussing the structure and properties of solids. But, at intervals, I keep thinking about the dating site. I was eager to reach home so I could look it up. Determined to find love wherever it was. Tyler beckoned to me that it was enough for the evening. We recoil to our respective corners.

"Remember to check out the dating site," Tyler indicated to me.

"Sure, send me the information. How do I join?"

Lia started laughing. I thought that it was because she thought it strange that a grown man had never been to a dating site, but she had something else in mind.

"Go to the barber first, then take some nice pictures for your profile!"

"Cool, I will do it this weekend."

The two happy campers headed to their car holding hands. I could see the love fairy guarding them, creating a path where they can blossom and grow. As they vanished out of sight, I set out for home, thinking about the course I intend to take. I was enthusiastic about online dating because I witnessed the results. However, I cautioned myself. This is an effort to find love. It may work, or it may not. Whatever it was, I was determined to reverse my misfortune.

After leaving work on Saturday, I went to the barber. I asked her to give me her best haircut.

"I always give you a great cut," she said as she covers me with the cape.

"I know, but I want to look handsome this time."

The barber set out to create artwork. Hairs were flying all over the place. The sheer was on for a kill. Parting my hair with perfection to create even lengths. The barber was striking up different conversations while making an impact. After forty-five minutes, the damage was done. I looked different. It was magic. The barber created a handsome man. She fixed my beard to match my hair. I loved it. This was the best haircut I had. I thanked her with a moderate tip and left.

It was time for the pictures. Nothing could spoil the moment. The photographer treats me like a star. I was a model for ten minutes. Striking different poses while I glide down the runway. Appearing from the shadows to command the light. Depicting heaven from a distance where the spark of success was evident. These were glamour shots. The photographer uses technology to create different backgrounds. The pictures were hits.

I uploaded three pictures to the dating site. My profile was detailed. It indicated who I am and the type of woman I was looking for. I called Tyler and informed him that I posted my profile and he was excited. Nervousness starts to set in, but hope was leading me. Tyler told me to be patient and that I might find friends. This concept is new to me. It is like venturing on a blind date. Soliciting friendship from the unknown. Ignorant of knowing is on the other side.

Love has several phases. I hope to find friends. These friends will lead to something special. It is important to let the process play out. Impatience might lead to unsavory characters. Even though I was skeptical, it makes me cautious. I have hope. I hope to meet someone special. The hope of replicating Tyler's success. It is a world full of lonely people like me looking for love. Professional women and men who are driven by their careers and have no time for dating. I am ready for the world. Ready for any challenge.

The dark shadow in the night skies starts to dissipate. Depiction of stars appearing in formation. I can see calm. Was it calm before the storm? Whatever it is, I hope it changes my life for the better. I have a big heart. I have a good heart. For the past two years, I have been trying to fight loneliness. The door is now ajar. I feel stronger. Accumulating the will and power to push loneliness through the door and let love and happiness take control. I amassed the will to fight.

It is important to align my beliefs with my values. It is early days yet, but curiosity begins to torment me. I am eager for love. I am eager to find someone willing to listen to my stories. The hollowness in my dreams must be filled. The days were getting shorter and the nights longer. I want to be normal again. Ready to kiss again. I am ready. I couldn't understand why the threat of darkness was haunting me. Falsifying bad ideas into nightmares and taunting me every night. Sleep is no longer fun. It becomes a death sentence that haunts me. I need to regain my life. It is important to develop techniques to counter the beast that was bullying me in my sleep. I am afraid to go near the bed at night. I must be brave. I must stay strong. It is within my grasp to overcome the obstacle. Relationships are beautiful and provide levels of comfort to the people that I know. I am special, but not different. I want to enjoy the things that love has to offer. Somewhere in the universe, there is a special person waiting for me. I know it. I can feel it. The depictions are in my head, and I am determined to bring them to reality.

CHAPTER 5

A new day had dawned. Waking up with eagerness. Eager to check my phone, hoping to see if my life would change. To see if anyone notices my profile. I was left in suspense. My profile was as new as the day I created it. No one noticed me. I wanted a quick fix. Suddenly, I remembered what Tyler told me. I must prepare for the long haul.

Most of the messages on my phone were from Kylee. She had not seen me in weeks and wanted to come over. One message read: "Hey, Dan, I have not seen you in weeks. Are you trying to ignore me? If you are, it is not working. You know your lips belong to me. I own you. I demand to see you tonight."

The messages were getting strange the more I read. There were more than fifty messages left last night alone. I started to worry. As I was reading the messages, she was calling me. When will this end? It appears that there was no exit. I notice a pattern of anger in her messages. This is not depression. It is a type of entitlement. Kylee believes that she is superior. This was a mentality that she developed over seven years when I thought I was in love. I felt I was obligated to do everything for her even though she does nothing for me.

I need to wake up and smell reality. It was a feeling I never had. I was interested to do what it takes to make everybody happy at my expense. I have suffered inside for years. Caressing the feeling of disappointment and low self-esteem. Believing that love means surrendering your freedom and sanity to your partner in the interest of a good relationship. Going hungry while your partner had a healthy meal. Staying poor so your companion becomes rich.

Kylee would not stop calling. After twenty attempts, I decided to answer the phone. If sanity and civility are to prevail, I must stay calm. Whatever I do, my interests must be tantamount. This must be the day that I make it clear that it was over. It was a myth. Kylee ended the relationship two years ago. I am not interested in babysitting her any more. I deserve life. I demand a life where the warm embrace of my partner is equal to mine. Where the shower of love falls on our houses equally and transcends to falling on a single unit. The bond of embrace should not be manipulated. The compromise should be unitary.

The ugly truth of infatuation was disguised under the banner of love, forcing me to surrender to a false sense of security. I ignored the advice of my parents and friends to my detriment. I will not repeat history. History was recorded for a reason. It should be used as a guide to make better decisions in the future.

"Hi, Kylee, how are you? This must be an emergency why you call and text so many times"

"Did you not get my text the first time? I will not be ignored, Dan. I demand to see my man, to see my man every day."

"Your man, your man Kylee, you left me two years ago"

"I did not leave you baby; I took a break as there was nothing that you could do for me at the time. I was a successful model and could not be seen dating a mechanic." I could not take you to New York with me. The industry demands perfection, and you were far from that."

"Oh, I see. So, I am a substitute that you want to use for your convenience. To dump me when the tide is high and reuse me when the tide is low. Sorry to advise you, but those days are over.

I am my own man now."

"But why are you saying that, Dan? I thought I was your world. You know you want me, and you will take me back without hesitation. So, tell me what time to come over. I need you to cook for me tonight."

"Kylee, you are not listening. It's not going to happen. It is officially over. For years, you have used and abused me. You treated me like garbage, and I stayed because I thought I was in love. What a difference two years make. I have grown. I learn to understand the difference between love and infatuation."

"It is over when I say it is over. Who put you up to this? Is it your selfish mom who is always lying?"

"Leave my mother out of your mouth." I was getting visibly upset. As a method to demean me, Kylee believes that I was incapable of making my own decisions.

This was the first time I ever raised my voice while talking to Kylee. But she was so narcissistic that I needed to make my point forcefully. This was the opportune time to make my move. Although I know it wasn't over. I know I had several more hurdles to overcome with Kylee and I was prepared for them.

"Are you going to choose your mom over me? You are not serious right now. I will bash your mother as much as I want. She does not like me, and I do not like her either. If we are together, I do not want you to talk to her."

"I think you have crossed the line, Kylee, and this is where the call ends. I do not want you to call or text me again. If you do, I will block your number. I am done with your stupidity."

"You will see, Dan, you will see."

As I hang up the phone, the calls and texts continue to come in. After two hours, I decided to block Kylee's number. This was painful. I did not want our friendship to end this way. History has a way to repeat itself. Kylee blocked my number two years ago when she broke up with me. But, like me, I know she was not done.

I decided to go stay at my mother's house for the weekend in case she decided to show up at my house. I parked my car down the street away from my house until I got ready. I turned the lights off in the house and used a flashlight to get by. I heard a car drive up at my gate. I peeked through the window and realized that it was Kylee. She bangs on the door about twenty times. At one point I thought that she was going to kick it in. The neighbors heard the commotion and came to investigate. They realized it was Kylee, and they quickly retreated.

After an hour, the knocking stopped. I thought she left. I crawled like a snake to the window to see if the coast was clear. Kylee was sitting on the front step. Like a kangaroo, I sprang across the hall. I grabbed my bags and rolled to the door. Like a ninja, I glide through the air. I exit the backdoor and climb the fence into the neighbor's yard. Donald was my friend who I had known for several years. Once the sensor light at the back came on, he saw it was me and let me in through the back of the house. Through Donald's living room window, I could see Kylee sitting comfortably at the front door. Occasionally, she would make a phone call and then resume knocking.

I exited Donald's house and rushed up the road to my car. I was going so fast that I broke Usain Bolt's hundred-meter world record. I went to my mom's house unannounced. However, she was always happy to see me. I told her what happened, and she supported my action and invited me to stay for the entire week. I asked her if I should call the police and she said no. My mother believes that Kylee will realize in time that the relationship is over and move on.

The next morning, I called Donald. He informs me that Kylee spent the entire night at the front door. However, she left ten minutes ago. It gave me enough time to go home to get more clothes as I know she will be coming back. I was worried that she would do something irrational. Kylee knew where my mother lives and she knew I was there. She and mom did not have a good relationship because mom would complain that she was abusing and taking advantage of me.

For several days, Kylee would turn up at my house only to find it empty. She realized that this time was different. Kylee did not have many friends. She would abuse and denigrate female friends who were close to her. Anna was the closest associate she had. Kylee did not like to go out with Anna because she believed that Anna was embarrassing her. Kylee would often insult her in public and call her names.

I ran into Anna at the supermarket on Monday. I was on my way from work and wanted to buy some groceries.

"Hi, Dan, how are you? You look great. Are you working out?" She glides her eyes all over me. "I wanted to ask if I would arrange a meeting with me and Kylee. It is a meeting to resolve outstanding issues."

She greeted me with a hug. A hug of betrayal as the questions continued to come in fast. I could feel the tension. Anna was assuming the role of a councilor to do Kylee's bidding.

"I am fine, Anna. I didn't know that you and Kylee are still friends," I responded with a look of curiosity on my face.

"We are not. We have not spoken to each other in years. Kylee reached out to me and asked for a favor. I indicated that I would try. I didn't know that you guys were still friends. I heard that she dumped you for another man."

There was a long pause. I had to catch my breath before I

answered. It was no secret. The world knew she dumped me, and she was not afraid to brag about it. Kylee would remind anyone who asked about me. Days ago, this discussion would have been embarrassing for me, but I understand now what to expect.

"You heard correct. I am over her now. Disappointments in life make me stronger. Every broken heart can be mended."

"I am happy for you. Kylee didn't love you. I will tell her that you are not interested in talking. It might be for the best."

As Anna walked away, I could feel the weight lifted off my shoulders. The basket of confusion and chaos receded. My feet feel lighter. I felt like the mission was accomplished. For the rock of my life was crumbling. I manage to release the feeling of disappointment and move toward the light. It is a light that was recognizable. A realization that love can be a beautiful thing. I was not alone. Other people realize the unsavory character of Kylee.

That evening I felt a sense of ease. The storm had passed. The fright of heavy lightning and thunder subsided. Water from the flood was evident but was manageable. The skies were brighter. God was smiling upon me. The intricacies of love can be felt from a distance. It was like Independence Day in America. The nectar from the pollen was plentiful, and the bees began to make honey. I am convinced that Kylee got the message. The message was clear two years ago. I am not encouraged to cling to my master, but to find my independence. To suffer in the name of love was a farce.

Tomorrow will be a brighter day. It was not supposed to be this way. Love should always lead us in the same direction. I was hoping that if we couldn't be lovers at least we would be friends. To show my undivided love to someone for seven years means something. Some memories cannot be erased, but I cannot continue to be a slave to my stupidity. Memories may fade but a lifetime of happiness should be embraced. I had loved her, at least I think I did. I was blind to the malignant treatment from Kylee. It is never too late to realize my mistake. It is time to leave the past behind and move on.

CHAPTER 6

It had been several months since I set up my online dating profile on Emotions Dating. I checked it every day to see if there was any update. This morning, I received two notifications. I will never forget it. It would change my life forever. It was the first Wednesday in November. I woke up early that morning, wrapped in a blanket from the temperature change. My body was reacting to the weather. Maybe I was lonely. The element realized and was attacking my joints. It was the start of fall. I could hear the snow pouncing on the window.

It was glorifying in a world where true love appears to be hiding from me. The glow of friendship was scarce. Life is open to romantic embrace, but for me, it might take more effort. I am ready to find out what is in store for me.

I have two perfect matches. I was elated. My mind wandered. It went to a sphere where the reality of true love was realized. Basking on the beaches with seven miles of pure white sand in Jamaica. Wrapped in white and soaking in the sunshine. Caressing her arms while making intimate contact. It felt so good I want to continue for the rest of my life.

The first profile was Casey. Casey was a twenty-seven-year-old business executive from California. She spends most of her time traveling and working. The other profile was Taylor. Taylor is a twenty-six-year-old retail worker from Greensboro. I was anxious, yet excited. My emotions are high. I feel different. I could feel that love was in the air.

I reach out to both ladies and let the chips fall where they may. Life is strange. For me, relationships were scarce. I am hoping to get to know both women so the process of elimination can be easy. It is not my intention to date both women. My hope is for us to be friends and build a relationship together.

I called Tyler to share the good news and he was also elated. My expectation was so high that I wanted his advice. It was not an exaggeration to see the moon wait up for me at ten in the morning.

"Tyler, Tyler, Tyler, Tyler, I have great news," my voice was echoing with excitement.

"What is it, Dan, tell me? You are glowing. Did you win the lottery? I want a house, a car, and one-million-dollar cash." I could hear the chuckles in his voice.

"I got two matches on the online dating site. They are great women. I love their profiles. We have exchanged phone numbers and I am looking forward to getting to know them. Hopefully, I will make a real connection with one of these women."

"That is great, I am happy for you. The process might be long, but it might pay off in the end. When the dust is settled, we need to celebrate."

I was happy to have Tyler's approval. He advised me of all the steps and expectations. With an open mind and an appetite for love, I am ready to move forward. The sun was visible but appeared mild. The friendly skies were acting as an alley for the moment. I had the momentum on my side. Nothing could spoil my mood.

Brandon is not a fan of online dating, but his views didn't matter. As my best friend, I am trying to find a way to tell him. This will provide an opportunity to stop him from continuing to play matchmaker. We are supposed to meet for beers after work.

The focus of the moment is to develop an appetite that will parachute me to the next phase.

Brandon arrives with two female friends. He is not married and believes that life is worth living. His mantra is to date as many women as possible and love will find him along the way. We always argue about his reckless approach. I could not find myself embracing that routine. I love precious flowers and want to have one for myself. It is not just having a beautiful woman who I can water and watch grow, it is an ambition to wake up every day with someone and hope that we grow old together.

We spent the entire evening drinking and listening to music. I could not hear most of the conversation because my mind was preoccupied with the future. A future that will last more than one night. This wasn't my moment. I declare my hand early. The ladies thought I was strange. Strange in a good way. They thought that most men would cash in on the moment. One of the ladies joked that I was saving myself for marriage. It might be a joke to her, but it was my intention.

My jovial personality did not dampen the evening. I know how to socialize. It was easy to have innocent fun because the ladies knew my intentions. Brandon was deliberate in his attempt to put us together. He would momentarily take his friend away for long periods. But that did not bother me. I try to keep the conversations general. This was an attempt to avoid any intimate topics.

At one point she was staring at me in dismay. I was trying to figure out what was in her head. The feeling of intimacy was never on the cards. The game was simple. We were perfect strangers entertaining each other. They were Brandon's friends, and it was not my place to assume the connections.

"We are here talking and dancing for hours and you never

even asked me my name. It is a common courtesy to refer to people by their names. By the way, I am Danielle. There is no charge for it," she scolds me.

"I am sorry, Danielle, for my behavior. I did not want to give the wrong impression. My mind is preoccupied with personal matters."

"Apologies accepted. We met Brandon today and he invited us to join him for a drink. My friend seems to like him. Brandon mentioned that his friend would love to meet me. We just wanted to have fun."

"Sure, I do not mind hanging out with friends, Danielle," I say to try to point out the boundaries of my socialization.

"You are cute and all, Dan, but I understand your boundaries."

It was a tense moment as I did not want to do or say anything to hurt Danielle's feelings. I assessed that she was young and naive and got caught up in the moment. My responsibility was not to exploit her vulnerabilities but to show her the right path. Hopefully, someday, she might thank me for my kind deeds.

Brandon was not making the evening any easier for me. They were enjoying the moment. Never missed a beat. All over each other like the world was going to end. Mimicking the sun at the expense of the moon. Brandon is a womanizer and believes that it works for him. His rationale for his sexual actions was that life is short and he is making the best of it. I do not think that his argument makes sense.

He would tease us sometimes. Encouraging Danielle to kiss or hug me. Sometimes she defended me by telling him to leave me alone. It was a good atmosphere, but it was my responsibility to manage it. There is no harm in dancing and having a good time. I was convinced that we had a mutual understanding.

These were young ladies about twenty years old and dressed for the moment. The winter climate had nothing on them as their outfits were not conservative. Any man with loose concentration might have a problem with self-control. Alcohol plays a unique part in the evening's activities. It was like having spring break in North Carolina, although we were away from the beach.

I decided that it might not be a good time to tell Brandon about the news on my dating profile. He was having too much fun and it would spoil the moment. It was obvious that the ladies had had too much to drink. I offer them two bottles of water to break the cycle. They were talking out of turn and their words were slurred. They lay on the couch and quickly fell asleep. I retrieved two blankets from the closet and covered them as their attire provides no comfort for the weather.

As the ladies slept, it provided an opportunity for me and Brandon to talk. He was in a good mood. He was confident that he was doing something great for me. Smiling at every chance, he gets approval.

"Aren't they beautiful, Dan? I knew you would love them."

"Yes, I couldn't ask for more," I answered sarcastically.

"You did well this time, these ladies are keepers."

"I don't know man, but we will see."

I smile and nod my head in disbelief. The nonchalant way that he dismisses the conversation was concerning. For him, it was another day, another exploration. For me, it was another life being destroyed. Some people enjoy casual relationships because they are afraid of commitments. It is the fool's way out. Who am I to pass judgment on others, but that is not the way I want to take it? The path might not be straight, but it is accessible. I am willing to utilize the torch in the dark. There is a light at the end of the tunnel and if we have faith and perseverance, we will get there.

At that moment, I was motivated to inform Brandon of my intentions. I might not get his support, but he has the right to know me as my best friend. It might take a lot of effort but there is no turning back. I looked at him with glaring eyes as I pondered my next move.

"Brandon, I wanted to tell you that I met two great women online. We will get to know each other over the coming weeks and hopefully I'll start an intimate relationship with one."

This precipitates a long pause. Brandon was trying to process what I said. His head was positioned in the sky. It was as if he was counting one million stars and taking his own time. After about ten minutes, he looked at me. I could see the seriousness on his face. What was I thinking? I should hide it from him. He looked at me again with a smirk on his face.

"Is this what you want?"

"Yes, I think so Brandon," with a level of confidence in my voice.

"You know my views on online dating, but as your best friend, you have my full support. Just be careful."

I was left speechless. I did not anticipate this response. It was a new day, a new dawn. The love God had spoken. Brandon recognizes the determination in me to find true love. He wants to be there for me. This is what friends are for. To support my exploration at a delicate moment.

By this time, the ladies were awake. They look revived. Brandon decided that it was time to take them home. The temptations of life can be capped. For me, I can explore. It is not perfection that is required to achieve my goal, but effective execution. I wait for the sun to shine in my life again. The promise of tomorrow is never guaranteed.

CHAPTER 7

The cold weather was taking a toll on me. Waking up alone can be a disadvantage. When it was summer, I complained about the sun. Now it is winter, I wish the sun would return. Am I too greedy? Trying to confuse God. Complaining about all seasons. That can happen to a person who is deprived in love.

Today is a big day for me. The element may forecast a gloomy day, but I am determined to let the sun shine. After talking on the phone for months, Casey invited me to California for the weekend. My vacation for two days was approved. No one would dare to interfere with the seismic moment.

It was like a soldier going to war. My coworkers were my cheerleaders. They were wishing me luck on the battlefield. I have been preparing for this moment. Training in good and bad weather, learning all requisite skills in the field. I may not be a five-star general, but my mind was conditioned for the occasion. I was a sniper for love with the potential to take out my target from a mile away.

My mom drove me to the airport. She was worried but happy. It was a symptom of a mother's love. Believing that her child can excel but is worried that he might fail. She is a realist. My mother understands relationships and knows that they have twists and turns. I am a grown-up. She knows that I am a big boy. I am mature from my previous relationship. Like a larva trying to transform into a butterfly. As I develop my wings, my mother's job is to ensure that I can fly. Not just to fly for the sake of it, but to master it. It is a successful venture when I arrive at my destination.

The airport was crowded. I was fighting the people to get my place in the line. The ruckus of life can be difficult to maneuver but the reward is worth the try. Fighting the odds to catch my flight. Can airport security see my plight? Should they understand the mountain that I am trying to move to get to the other side? It is a constant struggle in a compact airport. The flight was about five hours. It didn't matter. My mind was set on the mission.

As the flight took off, there was calm in the friendly skies. The array of clouds marshaling my path and understanding my mission. Love might be in the air. I could see the birds patrolling the skies from a distance. Paving the way for a smooth landing. A ray of sunshine forced through the clouds. It is helping the pilots with visibility. The layout of the buildings from the horizon signifies the unity of purpose in relationships. It provides a layer of protection for people looking for love.

The focus of passengers humming in their language helps me to realize the reality on the ground. It is a constant reminder of my curiosity. I started to wonder what was on the other side. It is like a drum beating in my ear. The warning from Brandon just keeps repeating. Is Casey who she says she is? I am left to the element and live by faith.

I need to contain my fears for the next five hours. I decided to watch a movie. While scrolling, I came across this movie called *Persuasion*. It was a romance movie about a woman with a rocky past who was given a second chance to love again if she follows her heart. It was like destiny. I am caught up in the same dilemma. I hope to get a second chance to love again.

Even though we have been talking on the phone for months,

I am traveling hundreds of miles on a blind date. It is a dangerous venture, but life is dangerous. Casey is going to pick me up at the airport. That provides a level of comfort and security. As I watch the movie attentively, the flight attendant tries to beckon me for beverages. I was not in the mood to eat. I lost my appetite.

The most intense moment came when the pilot announced that the flight attendants should prepare for landing. I was shaking. The plane was shaking so hard that I thought it was going to crash. When I looked around, I realized that it was only me. I was shivering so hard that a man that sit next to me tried to console me. He thought that I was afraid of flying and assured me that everything would be fine.

I did not utter a word. Even if I wanted to explain my situation, I could not. I lost my voice. It was one of those moments where I was mute. The volume button in my voice was broken. Fears and anxiety had taken over my body. The man gives me a bottle of water and told me to drink some. He hands me chewing gum to counter my fears.

I could feel the wheels of the plane make a connection to the ground surface. Mastering the runway like a model showing off her craft. The skill of the pilot subdues the plane and positions it at the gate. This was done to thunderous applause from the passengers. It was the hallmark of a perfect landing, but it is the beginning of my escapade.

As people were descending from the plane, my knees started to regain strength. I was not strong enough to stand on my own. With the help of kind strangers, I managed to move around. I thought I was prepared for the mission. I was looking at every woman from a distance. The airport was spinning. It was spinning faster. I sat for a moment and beckoned to the man that I was fine now.

After five minutes, I felt better, strong enough to walk on my own. I was looking for Casey. Every woman I looked at resembled her. That should be a good thing as all the ladies in the airport were beautiful. But I did not want to approach the wrong person. I have a picture of Casey on my phone. I shouted all over the area and did not find her. I went to baggage claim and retrieve my bag. As I was heading to the lobby, my eyes came across a beautiful woman looking in the opposite direction.

She was a replica of an angel dressed in business attire. The designer suit stands out; a handbag that I had only seen in a magazine. As I walked toward her, she turned to the right. Our eyes make contact. I could see the first step of a perfect angel. Casey's smile lights up the room. It was like the sun overrun the airport. Everything for miles was crystal clear. With her eyes fixed on me, I was wondering if she likes what she sees.

If it was an arranged marriage, I would agree for it to happen now. Could this be love at first sight? I pinch myself as a reminder that I am in this for the long haul. A relationship is more than what I see on the outside, but for that, she passed with flying colors. I was looking for balloons and decorations. Casey deserves a grand introduction. As she was sliding over to me with a physique that complemented the clothes, I realized that I regained full strength in my limbs. All anxiety disappears.

How should I greet her? What is most appropriate? Several things were flashing through my mind. I was like the matrix displaying many images at the same time. As a man, I want to take the lead, but I didn't want to overreact. I was watching the actions of her body. The motion convinced me that Casey was about to hug me.

As she placed her hands around me, I could see the stars from a distance. It was the galaxy that was cheering for me. It was keeping the sun at bay so the festivity could continue.

"Welcome to California, I am happy that you could make it," she said as she squeezed me against her body.

I could recognize the words that she utters, but I hear them in the form of a song. It was Casey equipped with Beyoncé's voice. It was a smooth mellow voice with her words measured to display her intellect. The words were perfectly pronounced like a language college professor whispering her words.

"Thank you for having me. I wouldn't miss this trip for the world."

"Well Dan, I know you had a long flight, so let us get settled and figure out what to do for the rest of the evening."

I nod my head in agreement. All my fears were gone. If Casey was a serial killer, I would want to be her next victim. Almost everything about her was measured. It appears that she counts her steps while walking. To me, it was an attempt to ensure that they are perfect. She was confident in her approach.

I followed Casey to the parking lot. I didn't know what to expect. Soon it was evident. As she approaches the car, the veins in my body expand. It was a red 2022 BMW. I worked on cars for a living, and I know that this is the envy of the garage. This was a modern machine that complemented her personality. It was like a car show, and the vehicle was too precious to drive. This vehicle belongs in a showcase. It has no business on the road. It should be cherished, not scratched.

As I entered the car, it appeared that the leather seating was designed for me. I was the center of attention. This time, the attention was for a good reason. Casey would see the impression on my face. The surround sound was perfect for television.

"Do you like it?" Casey asked.

"Like, like it, no, I love it. This is a great car!" I expound on my answers.

Casey smiled. Her reaction was telling. She enjoys the finer things in life. How can I afford to buy her nice gifts? As I ponder in my head, she glances at me. I could tell that she was not disappointed in my appearance. She pats her hair with her hands and removes it from over her eyes, then gently extends it to let it glow. Like a mermaid, Casey flipped her upper body to make herself comfortable. I am a stranger in a strange land that is trying to escape the life of loneliness to torpedo into a fantasy of love. Feeling the feelings and mastering the moment. I am trying my best to be authentic and display a characteristic that she loves.

As I stared at her attentively, I was cognizant of the person I wanted her to be. I am trying to avoid setting an artificial bar where it was difficult for anyone to achieve. I hope to get to know her and let my feelings make the connection. I am eager to decide. But wait. Remember that the decisions are mine to make. Casey invited me to California because there is something that she likes about me. I accept the invitation because there is something that I like about her. Let the process play out by itself.

The car detours into a suburban community. I enjoyed the view. I observed all the popular landmarks. This was an attempt to see if I could repeat the journey on my own. I abandoned every warning that my mother gave me as danger was the farthest from my mind. I look at the horizon. It was a beautiful mansion. The manicured lawn was cut in a rectangular shape with the flowers carefully positioned. It had several types of roses that blossom for the occasion.

As I move from the luxury of the car to the luxury of the home, I can imagine the comfort that such an environment provides. There were rooms for all occasions. My luggage appears to be home as it blends in with the carpet. I was excited inside but maintained my composure. I was not afraid to shower compliments but measure my emotions to remain sane. The weekend is going to be long. It has all the hallmarks of enjoyment. Let me see where it takes me.

CHAPTER 8

It was a long journey to California, but I am curious to see what the expedition brings. I was marshaled to the living room and offered a seat. I was like a journalist using my eyes to patrol my surroundings. This must be where perfect humans are made. The scenery was screaming with comfort. The drapes were welcoming, and each square foot of the house was calling my name. I wanted to answer but now is not the time as Casey beckoned to me.

"Welcome to my home. This is where I spend my spare time," as she points out in different locations.

"Great home. This is a keeper," I respond softly.

"I am glad that you like it, Dan. When you are settled, I will give you a tour."

"Sure."

"I made the reservation for us to dine at a restaurant five minutes from here. I hope you like Italian food."

"I do not mind it, Casey. It is on my list of favorites."

"Well, let's go."

It was a long day, and I was starving. I realize that love is a crazy thing. Only love could cause a professional woman to invite a perfect stranger into her home. The friendly banter is good as we search for the unknown. We might be empty vessels with a vacuum in our lives, but our curiosity will dictate the future.

It is now nightfall and the stars are appearing. The moment

is so surreal. I don't know where this friendship will lead, but I feel like a winner. A winner who is willing to risk my life to find love. The love gods will be on my side and reward my effort. I can hear the bugs acknowledging my presence and the neighbor's dogs eager to meet me. Their owling and barking cannot be ignored. They were running from one corner of the property to the next. It was not in an aggressive tone, but they realized that a stranger was in their midst. The silence of the night was telling.

As we entered the restaurant, it was like royalty. Casey was known to the staff, and they provide comfort and security for the royal couple. I notice the way that they addressed her. It was like having the president and first lady in the area. As we sat, the waiter positioned the finest bottle of wine that was in storage. The price may be cause for concern, but the moment overshadows my fears.

The festivity was momentous, and we enjoyed the food. The steam could be seen from miles away and the smell provided its unique fragrance. The ambiance was tantalizing and was conducive to good dialogue. We talked for long hours and covered several topics. It was comforting to invite Casey to North Carolina to return the favor.

There were several points of commonality. It was obvious that we had loving parents and were both close to our mothers. Casey would mention her mom every chance she got. I didn't want to echo the same sentiment because I fear being called "mama's boy." I was trying my best to be myself; it was better to read the room. There will be enough time to introduce my mother.

I may not mention my father much as he believes that I am grown and capable of managing on my own. I disagree. Life is complicated and everyone needs guidance. The passion of the heart is a delicate flower that is easily broken. It should be treated with care. No one can teach me how to love, but proper guidance on relationships will make life easier.

After dinner, we went back to Casey's house. The guest room was prepared for me. The king-size bed appears to be mocking me. I remind myself that this is an exploratory trip. It is a trip in search of the missing piece. A piece of the puzzle that can be solved. This is a huge puzzle in my life, and it will require a delicate balance to solve it.

I took a bath in the guest bathroom. Casey provides me with a matching set of towels. These were made from special fabrics that appear to medicate my skin. The crystal water drops from the showers were special. They intensely massage my body. An extra layer of moisturizing lotion was present in the water. Maybe I was beaten by a long trip. But after the shower, I was two years younger.

After my bath, I transform into my pajamas. It was about one a.m. but I did not feel sleepy. The shower appears to have energized me. I turned on the television to catch up on the day's news when Casey came to check up on me. She was dressed in sexy pajamas; skin-tight shorts with a matching shirt. It is not an exaggeration when I say I was blindsided. It was like watching television. Casey was moving in slow motion. She sat on a couch beside the bed, and we started talking. We talked for hours until we fell asleep.

That night I had a dream. I was on my way to heaven to see my maker. My wings were large, and I was in a white onesie. Casey was flying beside me with smaller wings. However, she was flying so fast, it was impossible to keep up. At one point, she disappears. After flying for miles, I could not find her. After seeing the maker, he asked me for Casey. I didn't know what to tell myself. I went back to search for her, but the effort was futile.

I was sad and started crying. Suddenly, I saw a shadow appearing from a distance. The more I move to the shadow, the more the shadow moves away. I didn't want to give up the search, but the phone rang and woke me.

It was about eight a.m. Saturday and Casey's job was calling. After about twenty minutes on the phone, she informed me that she must go to her office for a few hours. Casey ordered breakfast from a local restaurant to be delivered by door dash. It was my first time waking up in California. By extension, this was the first time I have slept in the same room with Casey. Our physical distance was evident, but my emotional state was at peace.

Casey provides a quick tour of the house in case I need to find my way around. If I was a timid man, I would be in trouble. The echoing of my voice in the empty house convinced me that I was welcome. My mind tends to stray momentarily. What would it be like living in California? This might not be possible right now because of school and my job. I was so comfortable that I was willing to give up everything I have in North Carolina and relocate without a commitment.

Casey came downstairs in tight-fitted jeans pants and a t-shirt with writing on the back that states, "Catch me if you can." I am convinced that I see what I want. She was more beautiful than the day before. I think that she is teasing me, and it is working. The moment of truth is evident. My river dried for years and is now flooded.

"You look beautiful Casey," I say as I glance at her.

"Thank you," as she smiles with a teasing look on her face.

"Do not miss me too much, Dan, I will be back in a few hours. Just a heads up, we will be going dancing tonight."

"I can't wait for tonight to take you in my arms."

"We will see, Dan, we will see. Practice until I get back," she says as she laughs out loud and leaves.

I was breathless, but this would allow me to get closer to her. I am not a very good dancer, but I can marshal some moves. The day was quiet and needed some excitement. I did not want to go outside. It was better to stay where I am familiar. I surfed the net to see if there was any activity that I missed. After an hour, I decided to make some calls. Everyone was happy to hear from me including Mom, Tyler, and Brandon. It was a lot to share, and I was available to share it.

My mom was happy to hear from me. She advises me to take my time and get to know Casey. She was the opposite of Brandon. Boys will be boys. Brandon wants to know everything. I am a bit secretive and try to be selective in what I tell him. It was easy to talk about Casey. I was not short on adjectives to describe her. She burns a permanent portrait in my head. Any artist with a drawing pencil would find it easy to sketch perfection. Casey is a breath of fresh air. Mimicking the roses in her garden. I understand why God allows them to flourish.

I try to make myself comfortable in the TV room. Understanding my territory, I try to limit my movements. Should the pursuit of love be restrictive? The onus must be on the visitor to act responsibly. There is an element in dating for the man to impress his partner. It enables a willingness to act maturely and understand the rules of the game. The rules of the game encapsulate the ambitions to win. I do not want to win at all costs. I want to fall in love and receive my partner's love back.

I could hear a car approaching the driveway. Casey was back. She had three bags in her hands. It appears that she went shopping on her way home. I could not see the contents inside the bags, but the labels were from high-end stores. It arose my curiosity. As I help her with the bags, she inquires if I was good.

Before I could respond, her phone rang. Based on the discussion, it appears to be work-related. Casey beckoned to me that the contents in the bag were mine. This confirms my suspicion.

The first bag contains a gold watch with my name engraved on the face of it. It was fourteen carats with a shiny appearance. It was like a mirror. I could see myself. The watch lights up the room. It was beautiful. The second bag contains a chain with a beautiful pendant. It was a gold chain with a diamond engraved heart-shaped pendant with the word "friend forever." The third bag contains a new cell phone. How do I say thank you for these expensive gifts? I need to show Casey that I appreciate her kind gesture.

Once Casey ends her call, I express my gratitude to her for the gifts. I reached over intending to hug her, but our lips made a connection. I froze. She looked at me as we realized what had happened. It was like winning the lottery. Her lips taste good. It was a moment that will be recorded in history. It reminds me of my first kiss. Casey moves to the window. She was surprised that I kissed her. It appears that she was upset. I tried to apologize. She assured me that it was fine.

Casey was crying. I messed things up. Why did I try to kiss her? I was blaming myself for everything. I learned that Casey was hurt in a previous relationship. It allows her to develop an extra layer of protection. I try to console her and assure her that I will never hurt her. Casey was comforted. We spent the rest of the evening getting to know each other. Later, we went to a ball, and we danced the night away. It was memorable. We capture the moment. This was a moment to cherish.

Why does time seem to go by when I am having fun? The weekend ended, and it was time to go home. Could it be Friday all over again? I was getting comfortable, and Casey realized it.

She assures me that I was welcome to come back anytime. Happiness had ended and loneliness was welcoming me back to North Carolina. I know it was just a weekend, but I feel sad. I am sad because it was the beginning of something good. I am ready. I am ready for the next chapter in my life.

CHAPTER 9

As the old saying goes, after the storm there must be calm. I am back to reality after an eventful weekend. I can't stop thinking about Casey. It is the way that she treated me. I have never had anyone treat me so kindly before. The patronage was encouraging, but I am worried. Casey wants us to be friends and see where it leads. She is a great person and I want to be that one. However, I must respect her wishes.

At work, I tend to have more bragging rights as my coworkers believe that I am dating. It is not my intention to lie but I do not want to share my stories. The days are moving faster, and my college assignments are lagging behind. I need to take a few weeks away from my festivities to focus on my lessons. This means spending less time on the phone talking to Casey and Taylor.

Every evening after work I visit the library and spend hours on my assignments. I am committed to my degree and was determined to finish. I was doing three courses for the fall semester. After two weeks, I submitted all my assignments. I am now waiting for my grades. I have gotten limited hours of sleep. This weekend will be used to rest and refresh me for a new week. I was successful. The weekend ended and a new working week started.

On Monday, I felt refreshed and was ready for the day's work. I reached early as there were some backlogs. We work together until about five p.m. The manager was pleased with our efforts. I was about to leave work when my cell phone rang. I ignored it at first as I thought it was Brandon bothering me. On the second ring, I realized that it was Taylor. The mood for conversation was right. My appetite for companionship was at a fever-pitch. The basket of hate is behind me, and the storage talk of love has room. I endeavor to fill it. Let the tank overflow. It is better to have plenty than none. The forest might be far away and unrecognizable, but I am determined to make it my Mount Rushmore.

"Hi, Taylor, how are you?"

"I am fine, Dan. I wanted to tell you that I am in Charlotte. I am attending a training seminar and will be here until Friday and wanted to meet you in person."

"Where in Charlotte are you staying?"

"Days Inn by Wyndham."

"I think it is fifteen minutes from me. I am leaving work now and I will come to see you."

"Great, I will be looking out for you."

As I hung up the phone, I realized that this is going to be the first time that I meet Taylor in person. My drought in the relationship is over. In one month, I have made the greatest leap in seven years. It is time to enter the road of love. That winding road that leads to the Promised Land. As a mechanic, I see the car badly damaged. However, it is not unrepairable. It requires time and effort to make it workable. Time is on my side.

The trip to California prepares me for the better. It eliminates the nervousness and fear in my body. I was as bold as the sun. Shining from millions of miles but brightening up the earth. I drove to the hotel with confidence. Rehearsing my lines like a movie star, I wanted to make a good impression. It feels good. I want to conquer the world. Confidence in a relationship is everything. It is the foundation of a building. When the builder makes the foundation strong, people can rest assured that it will last forever.

I drove up to the parking lot. As I was about to get out of my car, I saw a lady in a red dress approaching the front of the hotel. She looked like a mannequin advertising clothes for Gucci. The breeze was blowing heavily. It was pushing her hair in several directions. Both her hands were busy, one holding the hem of her dress and the other controlling her hair. The element was trying to expose her secrets while enhancing her beauty.

Was this the lady of my dreams? This red dress looks familiar. How could Taylor know that I was attracted to women in red dresses? It appears that she works with the FBI and she read my file. Taylor was walking toward the car. My heart was beating fast. Wise people say that pictures represent a thousand words, but it did an injustice to Taylor. A true representation should capture about ten thousand words. If beauty is in the eyes of the beholder, I am the beholder.

As Taylor approached the window, she stooped forward to make a connection. I misread the room and thought she was about to kiss me. I closed my eyes. Patiently waiting for the love birds to chirp. Did they fly away? It appears that I scared them off. I open my eyes to the brightest smile. It was reminiscent of people advertising toothpaste. Taylor was so close that I could smell the freshness of her breath.

"The mystery man, we finally meet in person," she says as she stared into my eyes.

Taylor realized that my eyes were closed and wanted to wake me up. Her presence and appearance accomplished the mission. I open the car door. I may have stumbled. It did not matter because I wanted to stumble in love. This was one time that I wanted to play the victim. I am the patient in this movie. Play the part of an actor who almost drowns. Having Taylor as the lifeguard trying to save me. Performing CPR on me to save my life. My mind wandered away. My reaction was swift as I tried a course correction.

"Hello, beautiful lady," I say as I ponder my next word. "I am happy to meet you in person." I stared at her uncontrollably.

"I could tell Dan, as it appears that you are trying to undress me with your eyes."

Taylor laughed. I could tell that she was enjoying the moment. It was obvious that I was intimidated by her beauty. The voices in my head were conflicted. It must be the dress, as one of the voices claims. The other convinced me that it was her natural beauty. I do not want to pick a side. The verdict should not confuse me. I agree with both voices in a compromise to move on.

"I am moved by your beauty, accept my apology."

"It is fine, I get that reaction all the time. Let us sit at the bar in the hotel and talk."

As we stepped off, I was owning the moment. People who did not know us would believe that we were a couple. I didn't mind that belief. I felt empowered walking beside Taylor. My strength could move a mountain. The sliding door at the hotel opened on its own, but I convinced myself that it was my power at the moment that caused that.

We sat at the bar and were about to order. Both bartenders were rushing to serve her. They didn't even acknowledge me. Who would blame them? I would do the same thing. Taylor ordered a virgin margarita, and I ordered an 1800 tequila and coke. It was my shallow mind that should be removed from the gutter because I believe that her drink order was an innuendo.

The heights of her beauty were undeniable. I was proud to be her guest.

In circumstances like these, people tend to overspend to impress their guests. For me, it did not matter. I was willing to wash the dishes to provide for Taylor. She was a very good listener. I was surprised at the level of interest that she shows in my schoolwork. The encouragement was moving. Remember, Taylor worked as a store supervisor. Her passion for my struggles was a good indicator that we have a lot in common. My struggles were her struggles, and my stories were her stories. The depth of bonding was unimaginable. It justifies my feelings of belonging. This is a relationship that people crave. It was a relationship where two people can join to build a life. It is a step on the ladder that welcomes us to the middle class.

As the night wanes and the bar is about to close, reality sets in. Taylor had to prepare for her seminar the next day and I had to go to work. I was not ready to leave. I was enjoying myself. It did not need to end, but there is tomorrow. Taylor explains that she was grateful to me and indicates that she wanted to see me the following day. I was not surprised because I had already decided for us that it was going to happen.

Taylor said farewell and walked away. I was in her hotel, but I could not walk away. The momentum propels me to watch her vanish out of sight for the last time. There is something about that red dress. The sway from the breeze was telling. Each sway represents a sentence. Each sentence told me something. These were words that I wanted to hear. I was longing for the bastion of hope to fill my basket. I am ready to take the basket to the top of the mountain. However steep it is will not be a deterrent. I love obstacles. I will take an obstacle course to master my destiny.

I was in a good mood. A mood for love. I was playing a

James Ingram song on my way home. The song entitled "Just once" captured my feeling and requested to make the magic last for more than just one night. Making a compassionate plea to God to grant me a miracle. It is a miracle of a good life. A life that creates a precious flower and helps me to keep it alive. The fountain of life was resurrected. I hope to see the day when everlasting laughter returns to my face. Where the sanctity of love returns to my heart and commands its rightful place. I am hopeful that the day will come, and the magic will last.

It was an eventful day. A day that I will never forget. I am cherishing the remnants of my first date with Taylor. My furniture will be proud of me. Proud that I am trying and taking strides. It is not time for a victory lap. The race just started, and I am prepared to finish it. Not just finish but earn a gold medal. I deserve a trophy. My trophy case is empty.

I reach home at about one a.m. Even though I feel sleepy, I did not want to go to sleep. In my head, I was replaying the events of the day. I enjoy every moment spent with Taylor. The cicadas seem to agree because they spend the entire night blurting out Taylor's name. Who told them? Maybe one of them was there and filed the report. They would not relent. This seems like a protest. They deserve to be heard.

Should I go to sleep to see if the lady in red will appear? I was convinced that Taylor was the one. Was this love or infatuation? This was a good technique to allow me to get my rest. The lady in red didn't appear in my sleep. Instead, I had a dream about a snake chasing me. The dream didn't make any sense. I try to control the flow of thoughts in my head. It was like Netflix, going through a list of movies to select the right one. But every time I chose the movie that I like, the TV would change to a different one. This time a tiger knocks on my door. I never question my dream in the middle of my sleep. This time was different. My dream was disobedient. It brought a tiger to my door. The tiger knocked hoping that I would open the door. She intended to devour me. I didn't fall for her trap. I stayed inside until morning.

What was the meaning of this? Did I eat late? This was a bar talk from my mother that late food tends to manipulate your thought process. Taylor did not appear in my dream. Could the clairvoyant indicate that the tiger was Taylor? I would not accept the concept. I believe that life is destiny and love was formed through that process. I am ready to ignore the nightmare and find the missing link that makes sense in my life.

CHAPTER 10

The next day I left work ten minutes early. I went to the flower shop and got a bouquet of roses. Five stalks of red flowers represent Taylor's dress. The graphic of her beauty must be showcased in North Carolina. For myself, I place extra effort into my appearance. I mold my hair with oil to emphasize the texture and sheen, massage my skin with lotion to highlight its softness, and bask myself in cologne so I could be recognized from a mile away. It was a way to step up my game. The distance to the hotel was much shorter because I was driving faster to reach my destination.

This time Taylor did not meet me in the parking lot. She was sitting in the lobby reading a book. Taylor's eyes were buried deep inside the notes as if she was copying all the pages. Once the door opened, it caught her attention. She immediately sprang into action. Taylor lunged toward me like the tiger in my dream and welcomed me with a hug. It was a minute long as she gravitated to my cologne and the extra comfort afforded by the lotion.

"Thank you for coming back," she says as she continues to enjoy the ambiance. "I was thinking about you today. I enjoyed the time we spent yesterday."

"These are for you," I say as I surveil her entire body. Her compliment also bolsters my action. "I wouldn't miss this for the world."

"Thank you for the flowers, they are beautiful."

Taylor places the flowers to her nose and smells them. The reaction was breathtaking. It was as if I could see the smell of the red roses making a connection to her innocence. Taylor closed her eyes in a mediatory tone with her face raised to the sky. I could hear a deep breath almost like a Yoga lesson. She repeated her actions and then seductively looked at me.

"I love them, Dan, these are my favorite. I love a man with taste and class."

"You are always welcome, Taylor."

By this time, Taylor hugs me again and places a kiss on my right cheek. I appear to black out for two seconds. Small stars were coming from my head and goose pimples filled my entire body. I am having a stroke. The right side of my face was numb. I want to preserve the evidence. I am not washing this side of my face for another week.

As we sat in the lobby, my confidence reached fever-pitch. It was easy to formulate a discussion. I was using a teleprompter as the discussion was flowing like the Mississippi River. Normality must be restored. I am the master of ceremony. I am trying to cultivate a climate where the commonality in personality can coincide.

"How was your day, Taylor?"

"Very good, I cannot complain. What about yours?"

"Today was busy and I got a lot done. I couldn't wait for the day to end to come to see you."

"Oh! That is so sweet of you to say, Dan."

Taylor blushed as I showered her with compliments. The mood was good. She would smile and rest her hands on my shoulders occasionally. It was a real friendship. Taylor wanted to know in detail every aspect of my day. It didn't seem to weird her out. She listened attentively to every detail of my story.

Occasionally, Taylor would make recommendations on how to improve some situations.

I was at ease. I crossed my legs on occasion to show my comfort level. Laughing at every joke that Taylor gives and getting the same for mine. I can imagine a life with Taylor. The music of love is playing. Whoever the author was, the song seems to fit the moment. I have generated extra energy. We seem to be drinking the same cool-aid. Taylor speaks in detail about the type of man that she is looking for in her life. It is a man who understands her needs and is willing to fulfill them. He must be someone with a vision. An appetite for success. Someone willing to form a perfect union and build a family. Her life has been emptied for a long time and the vacancy must be filled. Do I have what it takes to apply for the job? If I get the job, can I perform?

I listen carefully to Taylor's demand and try to tick off the boxes. Did I meet these qualities? Did my characteristics match these criteria? To me, Taylor was describing me. I am the man in her thoughts, and I must convince her. At times she would be silent and stare at the ceiling. She seems distant from the conversation. At one point I interrupted her thought process.

"Are you OK, Taylor? You seem to be miles away."

"Yes, I am fine. Thank you for asking. These conversations are a sore point. It brings back memories of some bad experiences. I do not hold them against any man, but it teaches me to be more careful. I do not want to make the same mistakes again, so I look for certain characteristics in a man."

"I understand and I am sorry for what you went through. I believe that people should take all the time they want to get to know each other. It provides a level of security and protects people from bad relationships."

"I am glad that you understand, Dan."

"Anything for you, Taylor."

Even though my mouth was saying these words, my heart was in a different place. This was a place that was ready for commitment. It was hard to go against her belief, especially for someone who had bad experiences with relationships. Life is not always about me. Sometimes I need to sacrifice my self-interest for the betterment of others. It was a painful move and one that I might regret. But, in the end, I think I did the right thing.

Taylor was vulnerable and at a difficult point in her life. She was looking for a stabilizer and not a disrupter. I do not want to be the person to disrupt a vulnerable soul. I want to help. I want to make her better. The life I crave is to provide stability and happiness to a deserving flower. A flower that withstands the test of time and can be molded to perfection. The water might be deep, but it is worth the risk. I will win her heart and gain her trust. Only time will tell.

This is a getting-to-know-you session. We might be wide strangers but the passion for soulmates makes us appear closer. Taylor sought my shoulders for comfort, and I offered them for nothing in return. I am a strong man. Every day the tide of loneliness seems to fade. At the beginning of the year, the line of loneliness was thick. As time progressed, the lines began to fade. I will mow the lawn every day to eliminate the weeds because the beauty of the grass must be manifested.

Taylor confides in me about the types of secrets that only family should share. I know I have a passion for dialogue, but this is different. To divulge techniques for finding the key to a broken heart is risky. What did she see in me? I am thirsty for companionship and am tempted to make my next move. Her beauty is knocking me around like Mike Tyson in the boxing ring. However, I am not looking for a one-night stand. I am looking for a woman to spend the rest of my life with. The mission is to turn my house into a home, to convert my room into a castle, and transform our friendship into eternal love. Love is real. Life is not a fairytale where we can wish for perfection, and it is achieved. Love can manifest through the kindness that we share and the goodness in our hearts. I am not perfect, not exemplary, but designed with a good heart. I will treat her the way I want to be treated.

Tonight was more sentimental. The passion for dialogue brought us to a place where the mood was dull, but our intentions were genuine. Taylor gave me a picture that she took on her last birthday. This was a trophy. I will store it in my wallet. She thanked me for being there for her. It was also good for me. I feel comfortable telling her anything.

Outside it was about forty degrees and I was hoping for Taylor to feel sorry for me and ask me to stay. We talked about the temperature and how terrible it was this time of the year. I expressed my regrets for not having any company to keep me warm. Taylor was smart. She knew exactly what I was trying to do. I could see the impression on her face. The more I echo my vulnerability to the weather, the more she inserts a new topic into the discussion. That offer did not come. We depart for the evening and plan for the next night. It was not just the next night, but it would be the last night that she would be in Charlotte.

As I hug her goodnight, the extra strength causes me to pull her closer to me. Taylor almost lost her balance, but my arm was there to catch her. She burst into laughter.

"You are the hero of your own mistake," she jeered me jokingly.

"You gained extra strength. Where did that come from?"

"Your presence is a source of strength, Taylor."

"I am glad that I could help, Dan. I will catch my breath as soon as you let me go."

"Oh, sorry," I say as I released her from my grip. It felt good, I didn't want to let go.

As I depart, the routine repeats itself. I felt like a married man leaving my family to go on a trip to a foreign country. Loneliness begins to converge in my path. I could see the darkness protruding in the light. Trying its best to dominate the night sky. I just spent the evening with a beautiful woman. Shouldn't I feel better? I know what happened and it is a good thing. Companionship is beginning to be a part of my existence and my subconscious starts to alert me to the changes. It might be risky, but I am willing to work hard to maintain my sanity.

The final night had fast approached, and I was there for the farewell ceremony. Taylor was busy getting things together to go back to Greensboro the next morning. I was there on a buddy pass hoping that she would find some time for me. Watching all the festivities made me realize that she lives only two hours from me. Most of her coworkers were in the conference room socializing. I was invited but did not feel comfortable. I would be the only person in the room that did not work for the retail chain.

I sat at the bar for the remainder of the evening. I was not in the mood to drink; it would be weird to sit there. I ordered a Bud Light and was entertaining myself. The bartender keeps checking on me every five minutes. At one point I was getting annoyed. I got the impression that he was jeering at me. I was not in the mood for patronage, but I maintained my composure.

Taylor came over to check on me. She explains that the function might finish in another thirty minutes. I know she was just saying that to make me feel better. She went back to join them. That thirty minutes turned into two hours. It was getting late and there was no sign of her. It was getting late, but I did not want to leave. It took me four hours to drink three beers. I had to quit because I was going to drive home. I just want to see her to say goodbye.

At one a.m., the patrons were pouring out of the conference room and heading to their respective rooms. Taylor finally came over and sat beside me. It was evident that she was tired. She was losing concentration. The evening's activities took a toll on her. I wanted to talk but I could not let her suffer any more. I suggested that she get some rest and she agreed. Taylor assured me that my invitation to Greensboro was welcome anytime. I hugged her and she departed.

CHAPTER 11

It has been the adventure of a lifetime to have two great friends in my life. The luxury of getting to know them and allowing destiny to dictate the next move. My itinerary is overbooked. From working all day, doing schoolwork in the evening, and talking to my friends on the phone at night, I am oversubscribed. It is like having too many channels on my TV, I cannot find the time to watch them.

The fall semester will end in one week and I am looking forward to the break. I promised my parents that I would spend Christmas with them. I like the festivities. This time of the year my mother cooks for the entire family. I am entitled to invite one guest, but I am conflicted. My mother has a policy about female guests. She believes that only women we are dating with the hope of pursuing a serious relationship we can take to the family dinner. My brother, Berkley, is older than me and has been married for ten years. He has been the center of attention for the past six years.

I am dating two beautiful women but do not know where the friendship will lead. This year, I will invite Brandon as usual. I have purchased a new microwave oven for my mom and a leather coat for my father. My brother likes movies, so I got him a home theater system with modern surround sound. We are a close-knit family and repeat this tradition every year.

I am trying to find Christmas presents to send to Taylor and Casey. It is easier to find presents for women because I try to find something that complements their personality. For Casey, I sent her a Rose Prick Decanter from Tom Ford's collection. Her fragrance stains my heart and leaves a lasting smell in the atmosphere. Taylor got a full spa treatment at her favorite massage parlor. She possesses the gift of concentration and enjoys long meditation.

The FedEx truck was busy on my cul-de-sac as my Christmas presents keep rolling in. Casey is on her way to Paris on a business trip and did not have the time to get me a present. However, she sent me a greeting card. I was not supposed to open it until Christmas, but I always break my rules. The envelope contains a check for five thousand dollars to buy anything that I want. It was the best present I had ever gotten.

I had a big box from Taylor. It almost blocks the front door. She gave me a winter coat of my favorite color and a silver bracelet. The bracelet had my name engraved on the back. It was specially printed to emphasize our friendship. The deed is sentimental and captures the daily discussion that we have. This is no exaggeration. Every day, Taylor calls to find out how work, school, and my family are.

It is Christmas morning and I wake up early. The snow was pounding the window and barricading the door. Like a musketeer, I put on my protective gear and shoveled the snow from my driveway. It was beautiful. The snow creates a close relationship with the grass and covers it like a blanket. It was cold but it felt nice. The milky white snow reminded me of my youth. That was a tempting time in my past when I would play in it for hours. My brother and I would make the best use of the moment. The memory makes me sad. Sad that I do not have anyone to play with. The vacuum in my life overshadows the joy from my youth. I am longing to make a snow man. I reminisce on the days of playing with my partner. I was chasing her in the snow when I hit her with a cannon ball. It was just a snowflake. I miss the harmless fun.

At my mom's house, the festivity had started. She was up preparing the meat for the oven. The variety was telling. Several different types of meat are seasoned to the bone. The appearance and smell were tempting. They look edible in their current state. My mother looks forward to this time of year when she can bring the family together. Family from all over the country would travel to Charlotte to join the fun.

I started to help my mother with preparing the grill and setting up some tents in the back yard. My brother lives in New York so it is my responsibility to do most of the work. I like helping because it puts a smile on mom's face. That innocent face that would scold us when we were kids. That innocent smile would dress our wounds when we fell, feed us when we were hungry, or bathe us when we were dirty. My mother is half of my world. As old as I am, she still wants to scold me when I mess up.

It was afternoon and the snow was still visible. However, what was visible was the almost finished food. People could smell Mamma's kitchen from a mile away. The taste made an impression in the snow-like footsteps. Guests start to arrive. It was a happy time, but I was nervous. I was nervous because I knew that my brother and his family would steal the spotlight. My mother keeps looking through the window every time a car approaches. I know she was looking for Berkley. Did she miss her grandchildren, her daughter-in-law, or did she miss her son? Whatever it was, I pray that one day I can share the spotlight with my brother parading my own family. It would be a dream come through. A dream of having a beautiful wife and children. It is a hope of turning the tide of misfortune and reveling in the sea of success.

Suddenly, a white car drove up the driveway. As the door opened, I could see the designer boots making their grand appearance in the snow. Like a predator, it crushes the ice to show its dominance. The leather coat complements the boots. It was Berkley making a grand appearance at the Christmas dinner again. The driver opens the left passenger door, and a lady appears with two beautiful children. It was Jasmine, Berkley's wife, and his children. The day's activities stopped as everyone's attention was on them. My mother rushed outside in the cold to meet them. I could see the joy on her face. It was the coming of the second king. It was the royal family, and everyone was laying the red carpet for them. They adore them.

While the royal family has been crowned, I pretend to be busy. I think this was overkill. They are a great family, but the celebration was too extreme. I am happy for my brother but sad for myself. I am sad because his success highlights my failure. This should not be. Life should be designed where every family member is acknowledged whatever their status. However, this is not so. The results of love are beautiful and should be celebrated. It is not a measure of success but a part of God's creation that should be manifested. It may not be my time and that is OK. Life is a revolving door where love is not transitory. Love tends to find people wherever they are and whatever position they are in.

I am down but not defeated. I should celebrate the success of my brother and join in the festivities. Remember, I am human with real emotions. It is natural to feel jealous when a landmark relationship is on display, but my approach is wrong. To save face, I went outside to greet my big brother and his family. Berkley knows the mood in the room and enjoys the spotlight. I will give him his dues. Every dog will have their day. I will not feel depressed, but it did not stop me from thinking about happy times.

As Berkley placed his right hand around my shoulder to hug me, I could feel his insincerity. For him, it is like a competition, and he is winning. He rubs my head in a scolding manner like a big brother grubbing his sibling. I could read the questions on his lips before he asked them.

"Little brother, where is your girl?" he jeered me.

"We broke up, but I am good now," I embarrassingly answered him.

"Are you dating, Dan?"

"Yes."

"When can I meet her? What is her name?"

"You will know in time."

I could tell that Berkley did not believe me. However, I did not want to call any name as I do not know what the future held. This is his moment so let him enjoy it. My life is taking shape and I didn't care what he thinks. One day I will get my revenge. It is not about revenge, but about love. I will take my time to find a woman that will complete me. I will not be pressured to accept anyone that comes my way.

I wanted an excuse to end the conversation. I was lucky. Brandon just arrives and I left to greet him. I was saved by the bell. This was the first time that I was so happy to see my best friend. He saved me from further embarrassment. As we entered the house, he did not need much introduction because he knew most of the people in attendance.

The dinner was ready. Mom places them in chafing pans to make it easy to serve buffet style. She asks for a minute of silence to pray. My mother asks God for the opportunity to have the family together and that he would continue to protect and bless us. It was a momentous occasion. It was beautiful to see family and friends having a good time. It was like a kindergarten classroom where everyone was minding their own business. For a moment, I felt relieved. The attention was shared. People were reminiscing on the good old days.

The DJ was playing Christian music. This song had the room on their feet. The song is entitled "Take me to the King" by Tamela Mann and everyone joins in the chorus. It presents an environment where humble people were grateful to God for the moment. It was one of my favorite songs. I am a prayer warrior who prays every night for my situation to change. I believe that my prayer has been answered. Two great women came into my life, and I hope to have one be my bride.

It was time for souls. My parents went to the dance floor and demonstrated how true love is supposed to be. I was proud to watch them because they set an example for me to follow. Others join in the festivities. It was a happy moment. It almost brings tears to my eyes watching my parents dancing to "Dance with my father" by Luther Vandross. The way they looked at each other was telling. She lay in his arms as if there was no problem in this world, knowing he was her knight and shining armor. My father provides a level of protection that assures my mother that he has her back.

My aunt tries to get in the action by taking me on a dancing tour. Across the room, she displays her jockey legs while I fight to keep up. This is fun. It is what family is for. They should be there for each other in good and bad times. It was a time to put all our problems behind us and enjoy the moment. It was like a therapy session where the goodness of the people was manifesting, and happiness was the order of the day. No one could tell that it was winter because the activities caused us to perspire. This is what a support structure looks like. We had fun and regretted that it had to end. My mother was ready to plan for next year.

CHAPTER 12

The new year was looming and shined a spotlight on my life. I developed a new year's resolution. It was my sole mission that this year would be my year. This will be the year that I find love. Not just find love but fall in love and get married. I was ready for the world. Was the world ready for me? Only time will tell.

It is a tradition to wish everyone a happy new year and this year was no different. I got a wakeup call from Taylor which should be framed and placed in a show case. She always makes my day. Taylor understands my lowest moments and my deepest fears and always finds the right words to comfort me. I fear for her perfection. I do not want her to be my second mother, but a precious gem that I will adore. Relationships are strange. We search for comfort and security and when we find them, we feel that they are too protective.

Strangely, I have spent years searching for true love, but I have never put together a list of criteria for my soulmate. It is a lagging indicator, but I do not want to be caught up in the semantics. I think people should love each other for who they are and work toward a compromising end. Humans are possessed with different personalities and the ones that intertwine can form a perfect union. I am not picky. I am looking for love, not perfection. Humans are not mannequins. They possess feelings and emotions. I am not setting the bar too high or too low. I would rather leave the bar to the maker to a position.

I called Casey, but she was on a business call and asked me

to call her back in twenty minutes. It is hard to understand the availability of some professional women. Casey loves her job and is committed to making her company better. This requires her to spend a lot of time working. We talked regularly, but for short periods. Casey is a very nice person and deserves to find someone who understands her and will not affect her work. She is a busy woman and needs moral support to keep going.

Casey called me back with some good news. She informs me that she is coming home tomorrow and wants to come to Charlotte for a weekend. I think it was a great idea. I was elated. I am elated to have an honored guest at my home.

"What do you have in store for me for the new year?" she says as she took a deep breath.

"The world of happiness, Casey. I have been doing some reflection and wanted an opportunity to show you that I am the right person for you. I know that you are busy with your work, and I understand. I also know that you fear committed relationships, but if you give me a chance, I will prove to you that I am the missing link in your life."

"That is so sweet of you to say, but, but…" Casey searches for words.

"But what? I give you my word that you have nothing to worry about." The emotions were evident in my voice. I do not want to sound desperate, but I want to express how I feel.

"But I don't know. I do not know if I am ready for this. I am scared, Dan. I have known you for over a year. I trust you. I invite you to my home. I know you are a nice person, but I am scared." Casey paused. "I am a middle-aged woman who is at a vulnerable stage and is afraid to start over. I am afraid of another broken heart." I could hear her heart beating heavily through the phone.

"Casey, I understand your concern and you have every right

to be afraid, but I am not that guy. I am not any man," I say. The situation calls for me to be more convincing and I try to achieve that goal. Did I push too hard? My effort should not be seen as forcing her again her will. This is a slippery slope.

"I will think about it and let you know," Casey informs me.

"Take your time, I am here for you." I try to show maturity and understanding. The situation is getting tense. Am I getting through to her, or am I upsetting her? It is a question that must be considered going forward.

"I have to go, but I will think about it," Casey whispered as she hung up.

In my mind, I was confused; in my heart, I felt good. My heart is telling me that I have made progress in moving the relationship to the next level. My mind is more cautious than my heart. Several questions are swirling in the air. What if she says no? If Casey's answer is no, I would be disappointed. I have an open mind. I have grown. I am prepared to fight harder or move on. What if she says yes? I would be ready to move this relationship to the next level.

As I was here pondering, Casey was calling again. Could this be it? My mind starts to wonder. My heart was relaxed.

"Hello, hello," I answered as if I did not know who was on the phone. The temptation to ask about her decision was muted.

"I hung up and did not say Happy New Year."

"Thank you and same to you," I said and waited in silence. My hope is to hear some good news.

"I took back some stuff from Europe for you. Should I mail them?" Casey sounded more upbeat in her voice.

"You can take them when you are coming to visit me," I suggested to Casey.

"I may not come before Easter. Are you forcing me to come

to North Carolina before that."

"Maybe." My mind wondered again. I was hoping that she would say yes. It was a gamble that I was willing to take. I hear the laughter.

"We will see," Casey replies with more laughter.

"OK, talk to you later." I hung up the phone, I realized that there might be cause for celebration. Casey might fall for my charm. The climate might be cold, but it didn't blunt my momentum. I am on fire. The new year started better than I had expected.

Something seems to puzzle me. I talked to Taylor every day for long hours, but I realized that most of the topics that we discussed were not intimate. It is not my intention to be different as there might be something leading the discussion. However, I do not want to change my technique of allowing my heart to lead these topics. The fervor of life is uncertain and the search for love is enduring. My life can be captured in a song, but the song must be emotional. If I had the power to choose the song, I want it to be R&B. It is more aligned with that of Mary J Blige. This would encourage people who do not know my life, and the relationship struggles that I face, to look in my sun, and see what I see. The world of love is captured by different people based on their angles and concept of love. Taylor and Casey taught me that love is more than physical appearance. How could someone hurt two of the most beautiful women on the planet? It convinces me that all men's priorities are different, and our happiness has a different meaning.

As the week progressed, I went to see Tyler to update him on the latest development. I need some advice on the conflict that is occurring. I hope to make the right choice. As I drove up to his house, I could see the love birds from a distance. Like Siamese twins, they open the door. It appears that I visited them at the wrong time. It was forty degrees, and they were dressed for one-hundred-degree weather. Their clothes were mismatched, and it appears that they had a hard time in the dryer. This reminds me of when I and my brother were about two and four and we tried to choose clothes on our own.

Tyler and Lia were laughing uncontrollably as they opened the door. Lia was hiding behind Tyler. The guilt was evident on their faces. I could only imagine but I did not ask what they were guilty of. They were sweating profusely so I thought that their heat was malfunctioning. I joined in the joke as I thought it was funny. It did not appear that they were laughing at me.

"How are your guys doing?" I say with a loud grin displaying on my face. For a minute, they could not answer as they were trying to console each other.

"Can you share the joke with me?" I paused and waited for an answer.

"I wish we could," Tyler managed to fumble out a few words.

"Did I come at a bad time?" I asked the question, but I already knew what the answer was. Lia laughs louder while her hands cover her face, moving closer behind the door as I exit my car.

"Are you going to keep me in the cold? Do you want me to come back another time?"

"No, no, no." Tyler and Lia answered in unison.

These love birds are my source of motivation. Young birds, always fly together. It is their method of keeping their relationship alive. For their relationship to kindle, they must keep the fire burning. Every time I see them, the fire appears to be burning brighter and brighter. My life was like the flowers in my garden. The flowers were thirsty. I bought some plant food and gave them a treat. The flowers are growing big and one day they will blossom and maybe bear fruit.

"Please come inside." Tyler finally invited me out of the cold.

As I approached the door, Lia rushed into the living room and started picking up some stuff off the floor.

"Sorry for showing up at your house unannounced."

"You are good. You are welcome here any time," Tyler answered. He moves around the house trying to pick up any articles that were overlooked by Lia. These are incredible friends because they inconvenience themselves to facilitate me. I am grateful for their kindness.

I update Lia and Tylor about my friendship with Taylor and Casey. They express happiness for me as they know my struggles. I point out the conflict and demand their advice on how to approach the situation. Their responses were surprising. They explain to me that love is blind and there is no right or wrong answer to relationships. Tyler indicated that they did not possess the power to see the future and did not want to intervene in my choice. It was their opinion that I follow my heart and hope that it leads to the correct choice.

How can love to blind? This is the most important thing in a relationship. The rules of the game should provide clear direction to people who are searching for love. But no friend wants to be involved in such a personal choice. What happens if they are wrong? It would be a betrayal of my friendship. They are smart people and realize that. As I put on my shoes to leave, Lia and Tyler followed me to the door. It appears that they were pushing me out. Maybe they were ready to go to sleep although they did not look tired. However, I played the fool and left. They earn the right to be alone.

CHAPTER 13

February seems to be my lucky month as it was bursting with activities. School restarts and I am trying to get ahead in my courses. It was my final year, and my boss is planning to promote me to a line manager or transfer me to the plant as an engineer. This was good news as I need the extra money to pay my student loan. Casey had purchased the textbooks for my courses, so I didn't have that to worry about.

After weeks of promising me that she would visit me for a weekend, Casey decided to come this weekend. The moment could not come sooner. I had three days to get the house ready. This is a project I was willing to undertake. It is also an opportunity to give the house a facelift. To me, there is a difference from having manly festivities at home to entertain a woman in my midst. I changed the drapes and bed sheets and the bathroom to life. This includes putting up a romantic painting of a tree with the branches making the shape of a heart. Within these branches were two birds sitting beside each other waiting for the sun to set. These birds represent the beginning of a new dawn. The dawn of a lasting friendship is moving to the next level. The branches are thick and sturdy to signify the strength of our existence.

In the living room, I purchased some new cushions with bright delicate colors that are compatible with Casey's eyes. Two paintings were placed on opposite sides of the room but appear to be adjacent to each other. They feature the sea that captures and adapts to the blue skies. On one side of the seashore were some huge rocks that looked like a high mountain. Whenever the rough seas smash against the rocks, it calms the sea. This was a moonlight paradise that highlighted the tumultuous journey from loneliness to happiness. The carpet mimics the color of the sky with two inches of fibers that are as soft as a mint coat.

    I intend to create an environment where Casey would be comfortable and is encouraged to stay. I had two bottles of the best red wine and two wine glasses that resemble each other. Throughout the house, there were air fresheners that represent a discovery set. In the living room, lavender vanilla covers the air, in the bathroom, midnight rider captures the heart, and the bedroom had scented young love candles that consist of burgundy rose, amber, musk, and balsamic blackberries.

    The love that I crave is intense. I might be trying too hard, but I aim to please the lady of my dreams. I am a quiet guy by nature, but my actions are loud. It is Friday and I took the day off to pick up Casey at the airport. The flight was on time, and I met her at the baggage claim. Here she was. The perfect statue emerges from the escalator. Her attire was more casual. The definition of sexy has been displayed and the dictionary was no short on meaning. Her mood was different. I could tell that Casey was here to have a good time.

    As I approach, I stretch my right hand to take her bags, but she drops them. It appears that she had something else in mind. Instead, Casey pulls me close to her and starts kissing me. The pupils in my eyes disappear for a moment. I could feel the soft texture of her lips pressed against me. The thirst for love was evident. She did not want to stop, and I was enjoying it. I could feel all the eyes in the airport beaming at us. Casey realized it. She blushed and placed her head on my shoulders. After two minutes, she released the victim. It was not a moment to call 911, but a moment to celebrate my fortune.

I picked up her carry-on and handbag from the floor with my left hand while Casey was using my upper body as support back. Her left arm recalibrates from around my neck and was positioned around my waist. It felt awkward. Not awkward for me to complain, but awkward to make the next step. As my mind was celebrating, my feet were relaxed. I am not in a hurry. I do not need to move. It was five minutes for the first word to escape.

"I am finally here. Are you ready for me?" Casey whispered in my ear.

"I have been ready for more than one year," I reply in a somber tone.

"I think about this long and hard. I pray for hours that God will guide my next move. I am convinced that I am making the right decision. Dan, promise me that you will not hurt me."

By this time, I realize the time, hour, day, month, and year that we are in. This is it. I ask for it, and my wish is granted. It is my responsibility to rise to the occasion. I am ready for a committed relationship. I am ready for love. I am ready. The more I say it in my mind, the more I believe it.

"I will not hurt you. I give you my word as a Walker that I will love and cherish you for the rest of my life." I convinced Casey of my commitment to her decision.

By this time, we realize that we were at the same spot for twenty minutes with people cheering us on. Casey loosens her grip on me and holds my right hand. I could move with ease. We walk out of the airport as the star of the movie. For the onlooker, the suspense begins. For us, we are moving to the next level. The next level of the movie is where reality dictates the scene.

I dreamed of this day. A day when kisses have meaning

again. When I can move from the shadows of darkness and disappear in the sunset. It is the frame of this picture that makes sense. The whole picture makes sense. I need to make an album. An album to capture all the beautiful moments that we just experience. The beauty of God's creation. A partnership was formed. A relationship that was cultivated. It is God's will, and we will cherish every moment.

I drove out of the airport parking lot with Casey still holding my hand. Her grip was tight. It was as if she had just discovered something good. Something that she was convinced was worth holding on to. Casey was looking for security and I was there to offer it. Her head was placed on my shoulder. The passion Casey displays tells me that she wanted to kiss me again. North Carolina law prohibits drinking and driving, but the law did not say anything about kissing and driving. I turned my head to kiss her, but I could not see. I realized that the car was slowing and swerving to the right. I sit upright and start to concentrate on the road.

I could see the desperation in Casey's eyes. She was longing for love. She was caught up in that moment. She was squeezing my hands hard and whispering unknown words. This was one time I wished I could reach home in the next five minutes, but I have twenty-five more minutes to go. As I moved to seventy miles per hour, Casey was kissing me on my neck. I am losing my sight. I am losing my strength. I was losing concentration. I did not want to say anything to affect the mood. The road was getting narrow, and my glasses were foggy. I fight the feelings for our safety. It was hard. It was like pulling a car over the hill while blindfolded. I managed to overcome the obstacles.

I remember pulling into my driveway. The mechanics of stopping the car were blurred, but the house door was open. By this time, Casey was facing me with her legs wrapped around the back of my feet. With her body balanced by my waist, she kissed me gently. I carried her inside. The scents from the air fresheners seem to collide. Each scent wants its turn to serve us. The candle in the bedroom wants its turn. They were burning with aggression, spewing threatening words to burn the house down if we did not attend to them. I am an obedient servant and heed the warning. Lightning and thunder were raging outside, but the trees were not affected. Flood rain was gushing through the community, but the houses were not affected. Heavy snow covers the houses, but my driveway was spared. It was all in my head. It was an illusion. The actions from the element were part of the celebration that my head created. We fell asleep.

We overlook dinner as we were not hungry. Food was the furthest thing from our minds. As I opened my eyes in the middle of the night, I was afraid. Was I dreaming? I felt so alive that the thought of it being a dream would break my heart. I need to convince myself that tonight was real. I was cautious, moving slowly as I look across the bed. It was Casey. She was sleeping like an angel. It was not a dream. The lady of my dreams is now in my bed. It is the woman in my life that I want to spend the rest of my life with.

I need to position myself as her bodyguard to ensure that nothing hurt her. As a guard, I should not sleep. The moment requires my undivided attention and I spend the rest of the night watching her sleep. Casey rolled over closer to me and hugged me with her head on my chest. Unconsciously, she found a new pillow. A permanent pillow. Love is a beautiful thing.

In the morning, I went to the kitchen to prepare breakfast. I wanted to ensure that Casey had something to eat when she woke because I know she had not eaten since the day before. The eggs in the pot were calm, allowing me to turn them without any hassle. I turned my back to put the bread in the toaster when I feel someone hug me from behind. Her soft tiny hands form a cushion around my waist as she massages my abdomen. As I turned and faced her, she was prettier than the day before. I pull her closer to me and kiss her. This kiss was deep, and it lasted for minutes. It is to show Casey that I appreciate her company. As she stared at me, I could tell that she was comfortable.

"I made you some breakfast," I say, the first words in hours.

"That is nice, but I have what I want right here," Casey replied.

"I know, but you need to get something to eat." I lead Casey to the table. As we sat to eat, Casey's phone rang. She looked at me as if she wanted my permission to answer it. I beckoned to her that it might be important. Casey went to answer the phone. This gives me time to place the food on the table. After a minute, she joins me at the table. She was impressed that I knew my way around the kitchen but also elated that I cooked for her. Casey enjoyed the meal and asked for another cup of coffee. The feeling of achievement and belonging was absent from my life for a long time. My life has a purpose. A purpose that will demonstrate to the world that love is a beautiful thing.

For the time, I am unavailable to the rest of the world. People who were tired of seeing me will miss me. Those people that hate me will start to love me, and those that encourage me will be proud of me. I am a product of determination. Casey's presence provides me with enough impetus to face the world. She relaxed in the kitchen moderately dressed. I could see her eyes surveying the surroundings. This is a moderate middle-class community. The views are beautiful, and the people are friendly.

Casey expressed satisfaction with the condition of my home.

For a single man living alone, I try my best to keep the place together. However, I went above and beyond to breathe new life into the house. The surroundings should represent my guest. My guest deserves an environment where she feels comfortable. I have a new baby. She is my delicate flower. I am glad for the opportunity to water it for the rest of my life. I deserve happiness. I have been searching for happiness and I intend to embrace it. I did not have room to breathe. The wind was absent from my life. Now, it is like a storm with enough breeze that can last for a lifetime. I will cherish every moment that I have with Casey and do my best to keep her happy.

CHAPTER 14

Today is not a normal Saturday. It is the day that I make my relationship public. Allowing the world to see the beauty of love. Promoting the unity that our friendship brings and enjoying the moment. This is not a victory lap, but I am excited. I am excited to face the world with my partner. I have many people to thank. I have so many people to call. This moment needs to be shared with all my family, close friends, and associates.

I need to surprise my mom. Casey indicates that she wants to meet my mother. She wants to thank her for raising such an awesome child. I was impressed. Some actions of women can tell the admiring characteristics that we need to cherish. Casey believes that my mother and father should play a major role in our relationship. It is like asking my parents for their son's hands in marriage. But she just wanted to get to know them. Family is a source of strength and is needed in troubling times.

On our way to my mother's house, Casey wanted to prepare for the moment. As she looked at me, I could see the query in her eyes.

"Do you think that your mom will like me?" Casey asked.

"She is going to love you," I responded. I try to assure her that she is the type of woman that my parent hoped that I would meet. Casey pulls out a small mirror. Her eyes examine her face for flaws. She could not find any. Her face was flawless. It was as smooth as a newborn baby.

"Am I too fat, am I too slim? What about my height? Am I

too tall, or too short?" Casey wondered.

I could not control my laughter. Casey was nervous. She wanted to apply more makeup. At one point she wanted to remove her makeup.

"You have nothing to worry about. My parents are the coolest people you will ever meet," I explained to her.

"I just want to make a good impression, Dan."

"You make the biggest impression on me Casey. You are beautiful."

Casey wanted to stop and buy my parents a gift, but I convinced her that it was not necessary. The aim is for my mother to love her as she is. To satisfy Casey, we stopped at Starbucks and picked up two cups of coffee. I explain that my mom loves a blond roast while my dad prefers chai latte.

I pulled up in my mom's driveway. No one came to greet me. They were not aware that I was coming with a guest. As I opened the door with my key, I observed my mother sitting in the living room reading a magazine. She looked up and saw Casey. I could see the curiosity across her forehead. My mom attempts to speak. Her lips were moving but the words were not coming out. She was playing it cautiously. Should I keep her in suspense? Her focus was on Casey. Let me set her at ease.

"Good morning, Mom, there is someone special that I want you to meet."

My mother quickly jumped to her feet and moved quickly toward us. Her eyes were fixated on the target. Like a mannequin, she did not blink. Mom was waiting patiently for me to do the introduction. She was impatient. I could tell.

"Meet Casey. She is the love of my life."

Casey walked over to my mom and extended her right arm. By this time, my mother processed what I had said. I could see her features change, moving from curious to happy. She realized that Casey was an extension of the family. Casey was her daughter-in-law.

"Nice to meet you, Mrs. Walker," Casey utters as she shakes Mom's hands.

The moment did not warrant a handshake. My mother hugged Casey and welcomed her to the family. "Call me Joan," my mother replies.

I could tell that she was happy for me. Her posture suggests that she was pleased with my choice. She beckoned to my father that he should come downstairs now.

"You can even call me Mom if you want." My mom shows her approval.

My father joins in the festivities and serenades Casey. It was like the Princess of England making her appearance in North Carolina. Having my parents accommodating the royal family. Roses were scattered in the hallway and the red carpet was rolled out. Two celebrations were occurring simultaneously. My parents were happy that I finally turn the corner from Kylee and continued on the straight. It was a road that was rocky and narrow. One that brought heartache and pain. The world of darkness dominated my life and locked me in a tunnel. There was no light and no end in sight. It was my mom's mission to help me through those dark times. She has every reason to celebrate.

The next reason for my parent's celebration was the entrance of this beautiful woman into my life. Their reaction was breathtaking, but a little embarrassing. They have so much admiration for Casey that it can be construed that they were surprised that I found such a nice woman. Casey was too good for me. This was the celebratory tone coming from my parents.

As I stepped onto the back coach to talk to my father, I could hear my mother grilling Casey. It was a long interview and the journalist wanted to know everything. Casey did not mind the approach from my mother. She was cautious because she wants to earn my mom's blessing. My father was happy too but seems to have a strange way of showing it. He offered me a drink. As I accept, he got two beers from the fridge, and we sat as a member of the same team. We have not done this in three years because my father believes that I should grow up and face my problem. He is no longer the coach of the team. He is a regular member. We communicate as two players training for the same team. He is a seasoned player, and I am a rookie. He knows the rules of the game and I need to follow his lead.

Mom and Casey joined the party. After drinking the coffee that we got from Starbucks, mom took out a bottle of champagne from her collection. The bottle of Dom Perignon was fit for the occasion because it was special. As she opened it, the loud pop was everlasting. It was like a cannon exploding in the middle of a war, echoing through the house in a salvatory tone. The remnants of the champagne splash in the air like a sporadic shower of rain. Even Dom Perignon acknowledged the moment.

It was time for the stories and the pictures from the family album. This was embarrassing for me. The album contains pictures of me and my brother when we were kids swimming in the lake in our birthday suits. It was hard to look at because it exposes my innocence. I was a child, and my innocence was proportionate to my age. Casey was enjoying the pictures.

"Come on, Mom. Do you need to show those?" I negotiated for them not to be released.

"We are proud of your past and will display them every chance we get," Mom points out.

Suddenly, everybody starts laughing. I know it was the

picture of me attending my cousin's birthday party thirty years ago. It was brutal. It made me look like a nerd. I was in blue overalls with a white cotton shirt. My hair was long. It appears that I did not see the barber from birth. Even though these pictures were hard to accept as an adult, it shows my transformation over the years.

We moved the gathering inside because the cold was getting the better of us. Casey was getting comfortable around my parents and was not afraid to share her stores. Sometimes she would curl up in my arms which displays a sense of belonging. She would retreat at times when she believes that it was too graphic. It was the respect that she has for them.

"How did you guys meet." Casey asked.

"It's a long story." My mother answered. "I am happy to share our story. It was the summer of 1985; I went to the supermarket in a small community of Lake Park where I live with my mother. I was heading to the car with six bags of groceries when the bottom of one of the bags with the fruits decided to give way. The oranges and apples were all over the place. It was like the Olympics; the track was busy. The young man appears from nowhere with a grocery bag and chases all the fruits and accosts them. As fast as they were, none could escape. The officer captures them and confines them to his bags. Then he took the other five bags from me and took them to the car. He convinced me to give him my number because he wanted to check up on me to ensure that none of the fruits escaped. From that day, he called me every day to check up on the fruits until we got married."

"This is a beautiful story." Casey was fighting her emotions. Tears almost fell from her eyes.

"This must be destiny because your husband was there for the right moment at the right time."

"Yes, and he has been carrying my grocery bags ever since," Mother boasted.

"Dad, you had game. That was a great move." I joined in the discussion.

"That is romantic. It is the hallmark of a good man," Casey shouted.

My mother was in her element. I know this was her time to give us relationship advice, and the champagne would act as a booster. It was like a reunion. It precipitated discussion after discussion.

"I know on the outside it appears that we have a perfect marriage. However, there is no such thing. We had our ups and downs, but we grew to understand each other. Life has a way to create situations to test out relationships, but we learn to be best friends, to understand how to forgive and compromise."

"Can you teach us your approach?" Casey inquired.

"It is hard to teach, but I will always be here to guide you in difficult times. The element of love is complicated. The characteristic of a good relationship is almost impossible to maintain. Some issues can be mended, and some are irreparable. We need to try hard to fix them, but we also need to know when to let go." Mom explained the mechanics of relationships.

The advice from my mother was deep and emotional but was transcribed in our heads. We were listening attentively because we want our relationship to work. Casey was attentive. The lecture was electrifying. How could love be such a beautiful thing and so complicated? Couples cannot live without each other in one moment, and the next moment, they despise each other. I am interested in building a lasting friendship with Casey and hope that it strengthened our love. I can't wait to see what the future holds. Great things await me.

CHAPTER 15

Yesterday with my parents was a Grammy award-winning moment. It signifies the start of our friendship and forecasts our journey. This was a best-selling movie. My mother collected the award for best actress in a motion picture. A picture that captures the intricacies of my relationship and provides guidelines for success. We sought her endorsement in this relationship because Casey believes that it was important to move us forward. It is a journey of a thousand miles that starts with the first step. We acquire the boots, and we will make these steps together.

Today, the movie continues. Our efforts are bolder than the day before. The journey that we intend to take is no longer singular. It is a joint effort to have four hands and two hearts combine to achieve a common objective. We discussed living arrangements. It was agreed that I would relocate to California once I complete college. I would keep the house because it was my first rodeo. We are in an early discussion with my company about transferring to one of its California offices.

Casey and I are heading to the beach which is about one hour away. My car is a 2015 Ford Escape. It is mediocre compared to the three-vehicle owned by Casey. Yet she was comfortable being in something that I own and work hard to acquire. She suggested that I traded the car for the latest Range Rover. I suggested that I would take her up on the offer on my birthday, which is three months away.

There is heavy traffic, but we were not in any hurry. Casey

sat in the passenger seat like a happy camper. Her seatbelt was fastened for added security. Her left hand was extended to contact my right hand. She was caressing the middle of my palm in a circular motion. Singing loudly to the song on the radio while her right foot was extended to the dashboard. This was a courageous move. Casey was showing ownership. Casey was comfortable around me, there was more to her action. She was showing the world that I am her man. It gave her satisfaction. She didn't need my permission because it was implied by accepting the role of a boyfriend. For me, she could do anything she wanted. I was like a father to his spoiled child. She could do no wrong.

I analyzed Casey every day and could find no faults. She was flawless. This was everything that I wanted. I accept the challenge of dating a business executive. It requires me to share Casey's time with her company. They would call her regularly. Even in the most intimate moments. Yet, my heart is not troubled. I guess love means giving up something to get something. Maybe, this was what my mother meant when she talked about compromise. I am not here to interfere with Casey's work but to support her in her quest.

The beach was full. The crowd was larger than life. It appears that people knew that Casey was going to make an appearance. There were people everywhere. Casey was in a black two-piece bathing suit. Once she entered the venue, all eyes were on her. She was the center of attention. Casey was a famous movie star, and every patron wanted her autograph. I was tempted to ask her to cover up, but I realized that I was benefiting from her popularity. The crowd, especially the men, was moving like a tidal wave. Every move Casey makes, they would mimic her.

Casey dives into the water and starts moving like a mermaid. She belongs to the ocean. Moving in unison with other fishes, the sea was making way for her advances. As she stood up in the water, life as we know it paused. It was a monument standing under the waterfall. The water was sliding from her body like a canoe boat racing in the Olympics. Hundreds of phones were out taking pictures. The images were branded in my brain.

It was not a perfect day for swimming because the temperature was about seventy-three degrees. But, for most people, Casey represents the sun. She was shining so bright that she provided added protection for others. Casey was enjoying the attention. Her smile was telling. She was doing Beyoncé's catwalk on the sand as if it was a runway on a beauty pageant. It was my contestant. I was her agent. It was OK for her to enjoy the moment.

The water will never be the same. Casey could swim and she was not afraid to show beachgoers her skills. She was a human submarine under the water swimming for several yards at intervals. Even under the water, her beauty was apparent. She was commanding the sky to take her shape in the water. Every time that she jumps in, the element would take her picture. I wanted everyone to know that she is my girlfriend. Nobody cares. They were enjoying God's creation. Who blames them? Maybe I would do the same thing.

After a couple of hours on the beach, the sun subsides and colder weather forces us off the beach. All good things must come to an end. The show was over. I was back to having Casey for myself. I was jealous but in a good way. People were acting civilized. They saw extraordinary beauty and were forced to acknowledge it. Maybe the sun knew the limit. There is always another day to have fun. Time to head back home.

I am glad that Casey enjoyed herself. She just put on a show. It was an interesting phenomenon, but she was comfortable in her skin. For a corporate executive, I thought that she would be more conservative. But no. She lives for the spotlight. Casey did not mind the extra scrutiny and that puzzled me. Casey realized that I was raddled.

"Were you offended by the reaction of the guys?" Casey asked.

"I am a big boy; I can handle it," I responded with curiosity.

"I love to show off my body. It is hard work. I spent a lot of time in the gym, and I do not intend to hide the result."

Casey moved her body in a boastful manner. Like a model, she flashed her hair across her face in a lustful way. Moving her hands in confidence, she placed both feet on the dashboard. She was making a fashion statement. Her energy was amazing. I love a woman with confidence. It was borderline narcissistic, but she earns the right to ply her physique. With a body to die for, it gives Casey bragging rights.

Casey is a complete human being. She was blessed with a physique that came from a 3D printer. Her maker had carefully created her for a purpose. The sculpture was flawless. I am attracted to perfection. This is beauty and the beast.

"Baby, I enjoy looking at you. You have my support," I responded.

"Thank you, sweetie, for letting me be me. Some men would try to control me and complain about the way I dress."

I was lost for words. If I agree, it will approve her license to do as she likes. If I say no, it will appear that I was trying to control her. I was locked in a box with no good answers. Casey is who she is and there was nothing I could say to change that. The best way out was to agree with her and enjoy the moment. Casey is full of life. I fell in love with the entire package and will not take it apart. My ambition is to own the moon. If some stars are captured in the process, they would be a bonus.

I do not want to live for the moment, but to live for eternity. That means getting involved with a woman who loves the finer things in life and works hard to achieve them. I believe in hard work, and together we can move a mountain. The elements are smiling at me. The days when I was in the boxing ring, when loneliness was hitting me around, punching me several times. Many times, I fell and thought that was it. But, in the last round, I got back up. This time I am winning and enjoying it.

The weekend is winding down. Casey will go back to California in the morning, but my life will never be the same. For the first time in three years, my actions and decision will be a collective effort. Time moves so fast. I didn't get to introduce Casey to most of my friends, but there will be enough time to do so. However, tonight I intend to make it our moment. It is all about us.

Casey was beaten by the power of the sea. She was swimming against the tide. Smashing her from left to right. It was a hard fight, but I believe that she won. I am on her side and my views might be biased. She fell asleep in the car. Once we reached home, she could hardly make it to bed. She deserves her rest. I tucked her in like a baby. Casey was mumbling something in her sleep. I was trying to figure out what she was saying. It wasn't clear.

It was still early so I decided to watch a movie. The moment was surreal. It was an opportunity to reminisce on the past couple of days. Things are going so fast, and I do not want it to slow. There is genuine happiness on my face. I could feel the emotions coming through my pulse. Sweating profusely in seventy-degree weather. Having sporadic outbursts of laughter. Nothing could break my spirit. God is on my side. The power of the creator is shining down on me. The house has never been so happy. The furniture joined in the fun. They had an extra sheen and shared in my dream.

I do not want to relitigate the past, but this moment might cause me to tread in any era. Love may have different phases, but it appears that I am placed high in the order. It feels good. I am with an accomplished woman who will help to mold my direction. The fortune of life is knocking at my door. I open the door and let it in. I liked my surroundings and decided to stick around. I feel high. High in the element. If I was a smoker, I would have a pipe or a cigar. One that was obvious that would enhance my appearance. However, reality allows me to embrace a breadth of mind and watch TV.

The next day was bittersweet. Casey was leaving for California. I knew she had to go, but I did not know that her presence would have an impact on me. She was crying from the moment she got in the car until the time she disappeared from the check-in line. I wanted to cry too, but I needed to remain strong for Casey.

It was raining. It was a symbol from God that this was a sad moment. The fog was heavy and required extra precautions. Casey was dressed for the weather. I try to console her during the trip. We are off to a good start, and we know where it is heading. However, life provides no guarantees, and we are the masters of our destinies. I was acting as a consoler in chief. Convincing Casey that it was the start of something great.

Relationships come with risks and rewards. We established some boundaries that would strengthen our relationship and keep the flames burning. Casey gave me a credit card so I could fly to California anytime I wanted. We seem to have things figured out. This will be a test to see what will happen after this weekend.

The fountain of life was crowded, but I was allowed to drink. I assured Casey that we will build a future together.

Casey checked in at the ticket counter. It was time to go through airport security. We had five minutes to say goodbye. Casey spent most of the time crying on my shoulders. She gave me her heart with one promise in return. The promise to cherish it and not damage it. It was a simple task and I intend to keep it. Casey is scared and I am scared too. We remembered Mom told us that problems will arise. What scared us was how we intended to handle any problem that arose. We might be young lovers, but we understand the boundaries of life. We are committed to the task and hope for the best.

CHAPTER 16

Everything in life happens for a reason. Sometimes we question our existence when things go wrong and thank the creator when things go right. People always cherish these thoughts. It is a regular saying of Brandon's. Who could tell that it could come back to haunt me? I wonder why people break each other's hearts. Were they always deliberate, or did it just happen by chance?

My story with Taylor is a complex one. We talk almost every day, but last weekend was different. I was busy starting the next chapter of my life. However, Taylor is always there for me, and I need to find a way to tell her about the leap that I and Casey took.

All experts believe that love is blind. It was that concept I embraced to find my soulmate. I am left in a bind. I did not answer her calls over the weekend, but I texted her to let her know that I was preoccupied with the weekend. It has never happened before. She finds time for me, and I find time for her. Am I taking her kindness for weakness? Taylor is caught in a precarious position. Her empathy and compassion are amazing. But she was burned by the blind emotion of love. This causes her to be reserved. She is afraid to get close because she is afraid to get burned again. I tried to convince her that there was no oil in my lamp to cause a fire.

Sometimes I thought that Taylor is ready for a commitment, but every time I try to get closer, she pushes me away. Her mantra is for us to take the friendship one day at a time and if we were meant to be it will happen. How could she show so much interest in my well-being, but refuse to commit to a relationship? Taylor would visit me once a month and ensure that my house is kept clean. She would bake my favorite cake and ensure that I am ahead of my school assignments. Taylor would talk to me for hours at night. Whenever I start a conversation about a committed relationship, she would change the subject.

I feel that I have a real connection to Taylor and try several times to express myself. It was as if she treats me like a big brother. About a month ago, I spent the weekend at her home in Greensboro. She lives alone in a middle-class neighborhood. During the daytime, she would drag me with her to the Friendly Center. We ordered two Nachos Supreme at Moe's Southwest Grill. I drew the chair so she could sit. I was eating and the meat was all over my face. Taylor realizes that my face was messy. She used the napkin and cleaned all the food remnants from my face, then used wet wipes to sanitize the area. I blushed. Taylor used her index finger to wipe the excess food from my lip. She was so close to my face that I closed my eyes.

"That's better. You can open your eyes now. I am not going to hurt you," Taylor whispered.

"There are some more on my lips," I suggested.

"There is nothing there, Dan."

"You need to come closer to see it. There is even something in my eyes, Taylor."

Taylor opens her purse and takes out another wet wipe. She turned to me and started laughing.

"Dan, that is the oldest trick in the book."

"What trick?" I asked.

"You want to try to kiss me," Taylor explained.

"No, I was not trying to kiss you, Mrs. Walker."

I was busted. My trick failed, so I try to make light of the situation. I assigned my last name to Taylor as a ploy to get her to laugh. This was an effort to build an intimate connection. Taylor would have none of it.

"I am Mrs. Walker now. That name should be reserved for your wife. It should not be thrown around loosely."

"But it sounds real. The name fits you, Taylor Walker."

"I like Taylor Pestano better," Taylor intimated.

I noticed Taylor had a bright smile on her face. Her smile always lights up the room. I realized that she was teasing me. As we left the restaurant, she held my hands. With her left hand lock my right hand with all fingers intertwined. She steps with confidence. Placing her head on my right shoulder as we move from store to store. Giving the store attendants the wrong impression. Taylor feels so comfortable around me.

As night fell, we went to her house. I was curious about the sleeping arrangement. I hoped to stay in the same room, but it was not meant to be. The guest room was prepared for me. This was my third trip to Greensboro and this room always haunted me. We played card games all night. Taylor liked the game, but she could not play well. I try to let her win to get her in a better mood. I wanted to kiss her so badly. It bothers me. How should I make my move? I was worried that I might do something wrong and spoil the entire weekend.

I looked at her and she looked away. Drawing her night shirt closer to her body. Covering any part of her body that might be exposed to the night light. That was my cue. I must respect Taylor's wishes. Any ideas of advancement dissipate. I pretended that I was falling asleep so Taylor would end the game and go to bed. She moved from the other chair and sat beside me. Pulling me across her legs with my head resting on a pillow on her lap. I lost concentration because I did not know what she was up to. Taylor was caressing my face. She was talking about an incident at work. I realized that she was putting me to bed. I fold up on her lap like a baby. She ran her fingers through my hair and massaged my skull. I felt sleepy, but she was still in a talking mood.

I could smell her perfume touring through my nostrils. Her natural body odor was refreshing. It provides an ambiance that was parallel to the oil on her skin. Taylor's hands were as soft as a newborn child's. It tantalizes my heart and elevates my blood flow. She carefully removes the grease from my face and attacks any dead skin that was lingering. A couple of love bumps on my face trying to elude her, but not for long. Taylor massages my body with care. I fell asleep.

I awoke a few hours later and Taylor was still watching over me. She was like a Goddess protecting me from all harm. Holding me in her arms like a baby in need of sensitive care. I realized that she was tired. It was obvious from the nodding of her head.

"Come on Taylor, it is time to go to bed," I demanded.

"But we are talking," Taylor suggested.

"We have all day tomorrow before I leave for Charlotte. There will be enough time."

"Just one more story. You are tired of me already?" Taylor asked.

"No, but I care about your well-being." I pleaded with her to retire.

"OK baby, I give up," Taylor murmured.

I held Taylor by her arms and helped her up. She braced against my body while I led her to her room. As I watched her dive into the bed, it was the first time that I got an opportunity to see her in her room. It was heaven on earth. The compilation of the curtain and sheets were in sync with each other. Her antique furniture provides a flavor that represents the class of a modern room. The carpet at her bedside was eye-catching. Four inches of fur was perfect for sleepovers. Before I could say goodnight, she was sound asleep. I kiss her on the forehead and draw the blanket over her.

The next morning, I was awoken by the smell of a breakfast omelet, eggs with bacon, pork sausage, and pancakes. Taylor was a mistress in the kitchen. She served me a glass of orange juice. It was delicious. I ate like I have not eaten in a week. I enjoy Taylor's cooking. Taylor reminds me that I would join her at church today. I prepared my suit the day before.

We marched into the church side by side. Making baby steps is like a married couple walking down the aisles. Taylor was clothed in a cap sleeve Wray V-neck summer floral split maxi dress with a black belt. It was good to see a mermaid walking on land, forming a complete motion with her hips in the closely fitted dress as she strolls along. My black suit complements Taylor's attire and makes us a perfect match.

The church was full. People were in the mood to worship. The pastor was preaching about love and togetherness. He explained that people will be loved when they love themselves first. He reiterated that people should not be afraid of taking chances. I looked at Taylor and touched my ears. I was insinuating that the pastor was telling her to give me a chance. She laughs and gives me a friendly smack on my hands with her purse. It was as if the pastor knew about us and was telling us something. Taylor listened carefully to the word of the Lord and nod her head in agreement with the pastor's sentiments.

Could this be a breaking point? If I thought that Taylor

would drop her guard, I was mistaken. To her, the message was a warning to approach life with caution. I couldn't understand her concerns, but I did not know her struggles. The beauty of love can only happen when we take the first step. That step seems farther the closer I get to Taylor. Am I doing something wrong? There must be something that I can do to convince her to consider me.

That weekend convinced me that Taylor feared a committed relationship. Now, I am going to prove to her that she was right. To someone on the outside, this makes no sense. How will I tell her that I am in a committed relationship when I spent the last six months convincing her to give me a chance? Taylor deserves better than this. Her compassion should earn her the right to know what I am doing. Should I call her and inform her, or should I tell her in person?

I texted Taylor from work and told her that I wanted to talk to her about something important. I suggested driving down to Greensboro, but she indicated that she would not be available that week. Taylor believes that I want to pressure her into a committed relationship, so she declines my invitation. Taylor called me just as I left work. As usual, she wanted to know all about my day.

I interjected. "Taylor, I wanted to talk to you about something."

"I will listen after you tell me about your day," Taylor demanded.

"It was good. I got a lot done today."

"What are you going to have for dinner?" Taylor asked.

"I planned to stop at Chick-fil-A and get a chicken sandwich."

We talked for two hours. Every time I try to tell Taylor about my relationship with Casey, she interrupts me. After several attempts, I decided that it won't happen today. I need to find the right time to tell her. She needs to know. I do not want to hurt her. The moment of truth should not be heart break for her, but a moment of celebration for me. I will find the right time. When will that be?

CHAPTER 17

The days are moving fast, and the nights are getting shorter. My birthday is fast approaching. Casey is planning a big birthday party for me at the Ritz-Carlton Charlotte. One hundred people are on the guest list, fifty family and friends from my side and fifty from Casey's side. It is an opportunity to bring both families together to get to know each other. The invitations were mailed two months ago to give everyone ample time to prepare.

The guest list for my side was done mostly by my mother. I insist that some of my coworkers, classmates, and longtime friends be included. Tyler should be the first to get an invitation because he makes everything possible. Brandon is like my best man at the party. Casey had contracted Taylor Swift to perform. She is one of my favorite soul singers.

As the planning of the party was in full gear, I had other ideas. This is the day that I plan to propose to Casey. I bought a diamond engagement ring with her name engraved on the inside. This is a radiant cut diamond that looks like a square with the corner brilliantly polished off. The ring has multiple facets that return light reflected in the stone. No one knew my plan. I think it is the right time to show Casey how much I love and appreciate what she has done for me.

The day is here. Casey and her family were staying at nearby hotels. It was a formal affair. Men were dressed in black suits, white tuxedo shirts, and bow ties. The women have a mixed of elegance from a laced dress to the shoulder. It was like magic.

Casey had on a silver iced cappuccino ballroom dress that was cut deep on the shoulders. The back was open with an elegant split exposing her right leg. It was magical as I watched her appear under the lights. I could see that fashion was made for Casey and she made clothes look good.

Everyone that I knew was there. My mother was directing the affairs to ensure that everything went well. Our table was positioned closest to the stage. It was a table for six. To my left were Brandon and my mother and father. To my right, was Casey and her mom and dad. I looked around the room. I was blinded by her beauty. With family and friends seated, the place looked like a wedding.

It was a large ballroom and spaces were reserved in the center for dancing. The music was playing, and people were singing and drinking. It was a festive occasion. One thing was on my mind—how to propose? I worked out the details in my head. I kept the secret to myself. I could see the joy in my mom's eyes that she was proud of me. It was my day. It was my time. I am finally appreciated by someone that I loved. The earth was turning, and it was turning faster than I thought. I could not imagine the day when someone special would throw me such a luxurious party.

The toast started. Several friends and family take turns repeating great things about me. My dad's speech was short but to the point. He expressed how happy he was to raise an awesome child. It was time for my mother. She was crying tears of joy. Hugging and kissing me as if I was six years old. But that's my mother. Her love for me was endless. She explains that she was glad that I drew up to be a good man. My mother asked Casey to join her at the microphone. She hugged her and kissed her and thanked her for what she did for me.

Brandon and Tyler tend to forget that it was a birthday party and focused their speech on my relationship. They make jokes about Casey taking their friends away from them. Brandon preached to the audience.

"He was a sad little man who was grumpy at work. I tried everything to make him happy, but nothing worked. Then came Casey and she turned his life around."

There was loud laughter and applause from the crowd. Brandon was in his element. He was getting support from the crowd, so he continued.

"Now, he is all grown up. He is happy. I do not have to babysit him anymore. We are happy to celebrate his birthday."

The mood was good. I was happy to see everyone enjoying themselves. Dinner has been served. Several varieties were on the menu. There was plenty for everyone. Berkley, my brother starts to beat his wine glass with a fork. He was trying to get everyone's attention. The DJ cut the music. Everyone was silent.

"This is not a wedding!" My father shouted.

"But I have a toast," Berkley replied.

"How old is my little brother? None of the speakers asked that question."

In sync with Berkley's statement, the DJ starts playing Madonna's birthday song. Then he cuts the music. It was like it was rehearsed. Everyone starts to sing. It was interesting because I know why they are doing it. When it reaches the part of the song that says, "How old are you now?" it is like the record is scratched. They sang it like ten times waiting for my answer. Finally, I had to reveal my age. I get up slowly, with a large grin on my face.

"Thirty," I utter softly.

The crowd helped sing so I had no choice but to shout out

the answer.

"Thirty, thirty, thirty!"

The crowd shouts and claps. They were enjoying themselves. The DJ asked Casey to come to the microphone. Her toast was reserved for last. The audience was interested to hear what she had to say. The room was silent. You could hear a pin if it dropped. Casey went on to talk about her fortune of meeting me and how determined I was.

"I am telling you, he wouldn't take no for an answer. If I had pushed him away one more time, he would move to California and protested in front of my house. But I was glad that I said yes to him. He is a great guy. But tonight is not about me, it is about him, so I want to welcome Taylor Swift to the mic to sing his favorite song."

The room went dark. No one knew what to expect. Suddenly, the voice of Taylor Swift was echoing through the speaker and the bands followed closely. She was singing "Begin Again" which captured the essence of our relationship. The light reappeared. Taylor Swift was on the stage. My heart was beating heavily and was escaping from my chest when she walked toward my table. She reaches for my hands as I stand, and she starts singing her hit song "Delicate." I could see the world from several different angles and in several different colors. It was the greatest birthday gift. She performs several more songs. Casey took my hand and led me to the dance floor. Everybody joined in.

The light in the room was electric. It provides a backdrop to the beauty that was around me. However, I was distracted. I had something else on my mind. I wanted to find the right time to propose to Casey. Casey has a poodle that she left with a sitter at the hotel. I borrowed the dog to enhance my charade. I tied the ring box to the collar of the dog. I know that when I signaled the sitter to release the dog, she would find her owner. A note was placed in the box that marked "Will you marry me?"

Several presents were stored to the left of the main entrance. Casey's present was the party, so I did not expect anything else. I was wrong. After dancing to "I Don't have the heart" by James Ingram, Casey asked that the music stop for a minute. She handed me a brown envelope and wished me happy birthday.

"This is my fight against you. I hope that you will love it," Casey announced.

"Thank you for everything," I responded.

As I took the envelope, it felt weird. I did not know what it was. Most people who get an envelope for a gift would think it was a gift card, check, or vacation package.

"You can open it!" Casey shouted.

An object appears hard. As I open it, I realize that it is a car key. My face lights up. I couldn't believe it. It was a brand-new Range Rover. As I announced it, people were cheering from all sides. I got their attention. Then, there was a loud bark. Casey's dog entered the room and was looking for her master. He rushed to the table and barked at Casey. The dog was telling her something. I get down on my knee waiting for her to notice the object on the dog. Casey took the dog in her arm and noticed the box. Her first thought was that something was stuck to the dog's collar. As she tries to remove it, she realizes that it was a small box. Curious about what was in it, she opens it. First, she saw the note, and then realized that I was on my knees. Casey opens the note and screams into the microphone. She was crying. People in the back were wondering what was happening. But those at the front quickly figured out what was going on.

"Yes, yes, yes, Dan, I will marry you!"

I removed the ring from the box and placed it on Casey's finger. She was still crying. This time, her parents and my parents join in the celebration. It was an emotional moment. Everyone was cheering. I was trying to console Casey. Her mom assured her that it was going to be OK. This was the happiest day of my life. For the wheel of love is in motion. Turning fast but heading in the right direction. The vehicle of love might be going fast, but I can control it. Life is good. Three years ago, I was heartbroken. Today I take the first step to mend my heart. Not just to mend my heart, but to combine both hearts to form one.

I know this was going to be a surprise, but it worked out better than I thought. It was a birthday party that was in high gear, transformed into an engagement party. I can see the look in Casey's eyes. The thought of being her fiancé was priceless. Her eyes glow through the lights in the diamond. It looked beautiful on her and matches her dress. Her hands looked different. She had bragging rights. It was a moment to cherish. This was like the start of the winter season. Officially, it is the beginning of a life together. The room looks different. Casey looks different. It was like the start of a pregnancy. The test reveals a positive result. Now, we must plan for the next nine months.

It was the loudest yes. Her voice is still echoing around the room. I get up from my knees and stand before Casey. My knees are still shaking. It was a beautiful moment, but anything could happen. What if she had said no? I would never know. I try to maintain my composure. I want to be a knight in shining armor for Casey. As I prepared myself, she starts kissing me. It lasted for about five minutes. She did not want to stop, and I was enjoying it. Family and friends were cheering. Casey's happy tears were evident on my shirt. I gave her my shoulders to cry on. She gave me her heart to cherish for the rest of my life.

As the party came to an end, people were greeting each other. They were happy for us. The event might be over, but a golden jubilee is brewing. I have something special to offer. Casey accepts it. I want to give her my last name. Tyler was happy to see that I moved to the next level. He signaled me with two thumbs up. This indicates that is work is done. His idea paid off. I need to thank him. There will be enough time for that. Right now. I have a wedding to plan.

CHAPTER 18

The time of reckoning is here. It is six months already. Love is in the air. The storm of happiness is blowing, and I intend to enjoy every moment of it. The day of loneliness is over. I am ready. Ready for the day when I wake up to someone special. It is a benefit that is appointed to married people. I can't wait to walk down the aisle with my beautiful bride. We intend to share a lifetime of love.

Casey asked me to accompany her to the bridal boutique to fit her dress. As we approach, we observe several couples scouting for dresses. I realize that love is in the air, and I am not alone in this journey. We sat at the front of the store waiting for an available assistant. Casey was nervous. She crossed her legs with her hands on her jaws. Observing other women to see if the style that she selected would be on display. Although she took all the measurements, she didn't know how her final product would look on her. She was quiet. I tried to strike up a conversation and introduce some icebreakers, but this did not work. Casey was focused. Her focus was one thing, and one thing only.

The store attendant beckoned to us that she was ready for us. I glanced at Casey who still has her head down. She was shuffling in the seat from right to left. What is she thinking about? For two minutes she made no indication that she was ready. Casey was processing the moment. This is the last time she will try on the dress before the wedding. Finally, she looked up at me and smiled.

"I am ready for this. It will fit and fit perfectly." Casey speaks with confidence.

"It will fit. I am here to ensure that it does."

Casey went to the fitting room with the attendant. They were diligent in their approach. I stood outside. After thirty minutes, an angel appeared. She was dressed in white with two large wings. In my imagination, there was a large white gate. Before the gate, God was standing patiently waiting for his daughter. He stretches forth his large hands to welcome her to heaven. Then, he was interrupted by a soft voice.

"What do you think?" Casey asked.

I looked around at the voice and I was stunned. The angel was Casey. The tailor carved the dress in Casey's image. I could not hold back the tears. Water was flowing from my eyes like a river. Her beauty had stretched beyond the dress.

"You look stunning," I answered. "I am the luckiest man in the world to have you."

"Thank you, honey. I love it!" Casey exclaimed.

Casey glided across the hall and into my arms. This was bringing the wedding day early without the pastor. Sliding the material into position as the dress shows obedience by following her wherever she goes. The boutique staff quickly interrupted the celebration.

"It is important that the dress remains in one piece for your wedding day. I know that you are excited, but you will have enough time to celebrate," the tailor explained while laughing.

They pulled me off my bride. It was not easy, but they managed to get the better of me. As I watch the staff measure and match every inch of the dress, I realize that they were striving for perfection. From the headpiece to the gloves were arranged in perfect order.

Casey was pleased with her dress. She talked about it for the rest of the evening. Everything was in order. The church confirmed that the flowers were delivered, all decorations were up, and the seating was arranged. We plan a three-day honeymoon in Paris. Everything is moving fast. It was heartbreaking to see families from both sides join in the planning to make this wedding a success.

It is the night before the wedding. It was a tradition for the groom not to see the bride twenty-four hours before the wedding. This custom was strictly enforced. I was staying at a nearby hotel, while Casey was at her house. My brother arranges a small party in the hotel room for me. I didn't know what type of party it was, but I was up with the sports. Brandon is my best man, so he was charged with ensuring that I stay in line.

The bachelor party had no women. We drank, played music, and reminisced. Suddenly, someone was knocking on the door. There was a voice shouting "room service." I didn't order anything, but Tyler went to open the door. He starts screaming in amazement.

"The party has just begun!" Tyler shouted.

"What is he talking about? We have been here for more than an hour," I pointed out to them.

There was loud laughter from everyone, including my father. I realized that something was happening, and I was left in the dark. A private DJ enters the room with his sound system. He arranged it in the room and started playing. By this time, I thought the DJ was the surprise. My mind was set at ease. I noticed the door was still open and Tyler was still guarding it.

The DJ was hyping the room. He stopped the music and asked us if we were ready to party. Everyone in the room shouted in agreement. The volume turned up. Suddenly, ten women skimpily dressed rushed through the door and start dancing. One of the women came over to me and place her hand on my shoulders. Everyone surrounds me. I indicated to her that I would pass as I am getting married in the morning. My warning was ignored as everyone in the room cheered her on. She was all over me, dancing seductively, but clean fun. I participated in the exercise because I know that there were several safeguards to ensure that it was clean and fun. Casey's father and my father were supervisors vigilant in the escapade. They were acting as movie directors dictating the terms of engagement.

The energy at the party was electrifying. I could see my guiding angels joining in the fun. My father was not afraid to show off his craft, commanding the dance floor with authority. One of the ladies tries to crack his old bones, but his age withstood any pressure. He and Casey's father challenges traditional orthodoxy. They were rubbing on the ladies like an octopus with ten hands, mastering the latest rhythm and blues like Usher in his latest music video.

My hands were by my side like a mannequin. My brother, Berkley, advised me to loosen up and have fun. I join in some close dances at the behest of my father. It was a tradition for men getting married to enjoy themselves the night before the wedding. The fun had boundaries. She put her legs across mine and faced me while sitting on my lap. Brandon pours beer on my head. It runs all over my body. The dancer uses her hands and rubs the alcohol all over my body. She pours another beer on herself. As the music beat, she was massaging my body with hers. Some people say boys will be boys, but the occasion was too important for me to mess it up. At one point, four ladies were teaming up on me.

I was also distracted. The next twelve hours will be the

biggest moment of my life. I was replaying the moment over and over in my head to ensure that everything was perfect. I freed myself and walked to the fridge to make myself a drink. It allows me to take a break. They hardly noticed me as they were having fun. My clothes were soaked with beer. I was sticky. Before I knew it, I was caught up again in the action.

I am in great company and their actions are innocent. We were drinking, dancing, and enjoying ourselves. I was watching the clock. However, Brandon was tasked with ensuring that I go to bed on time. I need my rest. After the ladies left, we were laughing. They thought I was afraid but handled myself well. It was like a boxing ring, and I just won the match. My father raises my hands and announces the winner. He was bragging to Casey's dad.

"I raised that boy. He is the spitting image of me," my dad shouted.

"I can see that you raised him well. He did not let us down tonight." Casey's dad added.

"He had some of my moves. I thought him those dance moves."

I was glad to see the camaraderie. It was an honor to hear my father praising me. He didn't do it often. He is a tough soldier who keeps his emotions hidden. I was the center of attention. It was a moment that I craved. My brother was happy for me. He makes every effort to ensure that I enjoy myself. I am a prince. Tomorrow I will wear a new crown. I will be crowned king. It will be king of my destiny.

At two a.m., Brandon indicated that it was time to wrap up the party. Everybody agreed. We joined together and cleaned up the mess because we knew that there would be no time for it in the morning. A lot of alcohol remains. This will be transferred to the ballroom for the reception tomorrow. We headed to our respective rooms. Everyone wishes me luck for the next morning. My father hugged me, rubbed my head, and uttered some wise words.

"Good luck, kiddo."

"Thank you, pops. It is good that I can follow in your footsteps."

Berkley joins in the hugs. It was a three-way celebration. The creator is smiling at us as he brought my family closer. I am convinced that I have their full support. Love is a beautiful thing, but it is sometimes a strange phenomenon. I might be searching for guarantees. It is not there. I realize that I need to face my battles. I took comfort that I do not have to fight my battles alone.

"You did it, little brother. We are so proud of you." Berkley explained.

"Thank you all. I appreciate your support. I could not have done it without you."

As they left, I lay in my bed in the dark. I did not want to be alone. It might be a good idea because it gives me some time to think. I felt like a shadow came into the room. I thought it was my father. I called his name, but no one answered. The shadow was by the bedside. I move closer to it, but it moves away from me. The shadow was asking me a question.

"Are you ready to get married? Do you love her?" the shadow appears to ask.

"Yes, yes, yes," I respond.

The shadow did not like my answers. It started to fade and move farther and farther from me. It eventually vanished before it reached the window. My body was shivering. Maybe it was a ghost. The voice sounds familiar. I am not sure. It appears to be Taylor warning me. How could that be? She has no idea that I am getting married. I agree that it was my mind and the alcohol playing tricks on me. After an hour, I fell asleep.

CHAPTER 19

It is my wedding day. I have not seen or spoken to Casey in twenty-four hours. We were mandated to reach the church at noon. The bridal party consists of fourteen people, seven men, and seven women. The men were dressed in black pants, a black jacket, a pink tuxedo, and a pink bow tie. The women were in rose-pink dresses and white shoes. We reached the church on time. This was a work of the heart. At the entrance to the church was a paper bell in the shape of a heart. It had different flower decorations around the edges. Inside the frame of the heart were pepper lights to highlight the shape. There was a bright red carpet from the entrance of the church to the altar. This represents the magnitude of the situation and a sense of royalty in our approach. A queen and a king are born.

    I stood at the altar for about thirty minutes before Casey's mother entered the church. This was an indication the procession was about to start. Casey's father was called outside. The altar was decorated in Casey's favorite color, with the floor covered with roses. The pastor asks everyone seated to stand. The band started to play "Here comes the bride." This was it. All eyes were positioned at the entrance to the church. My heart was pounding in my chest. It was pounding in excitement. Eager to see my bride. I looked with anticipation. Suddenly, an angel appears, accompanied by her father. The music played louder. Casey was marching utilizing careful baby steps. She was ensuring that it was perfect. The white gown clutched to her body with the veil covering her face. I recognize her by her beautiful shape.

As she strolls along the red carpet in her father's arms, I met her in the middle of the church. Her father handed me her tiny hands, covered in white gloves. I tried to feel the texture of her hands, but the gloves were hindering my judgment. The instrument echoed through the church as I hold my bride by the arm. I held the delicate flower and led her to the altar. With more than five yards from the helm of her wedding gown strolling by with the help of seven bridesmaids.

We stood before the pastor who took control of the proceeding. He rehearses the famous words that were accustomed to all people. I hear them at weddings with families, and friends, on television, and at church.

"Dearly beloved, we are gathered here in the presence of God, to join this man and this woman in holy marriage, which is instituted of God, regulated by his commandments, blessed by our Lord Jesus Christ, and to be held in honor among all men."

As the pastor continued, it felt like God himself talking. It was so surreal. The sound of his voice echoed through the church like lightning and thunder. Pronouncing his words as plain as day. Waiting for the creator to sound the trumpet, signaling a new beginning. Having us surrounded by pink and black creates a climate of calm and humility. The church was quiet, listening to every word the pastor says. It was like preaching a Sunday sermon. Having sinners aboard and trying to save their souls, praying and hoping that someone will get baptized. He was on point. The power of his voice was heard from miles away.

The moment of truth has come. The crowd wanted to hear from us. It is time for us to confirm our love to everyone in sight. The pastor turns to Casey like a force of nature.

"Casey, will you take Dan to be your lawfully wedded

husband? To love and to hold until death does you part."

I know what the answer was, but I still want to hear it. Casey takes a long pause. She took a deep breath and turned to me. Casey was still under the veil, and I could not see her facial expression. I have not seen her face in thirty-six hours.

"Yes, I do!" Casey shouted.

I just lost fifty pounds. They saw the pressure coming off my shoulders. I just crossed the most important hurdle in my life. I won the race. The hurdles were not high, but the distance was far. It was my turn.

"Dan, will you take Casey to be your lawfully wedded wife? To love and to hold until death does you part?" the pastor asked.

"I do!" I shouted with confidence.

Our commitments were clear and there were no objections from the congregation. Everyone believes that we should be married.

"By the power invested in me by the state of California, I now pronounce you man and wife. You may kiss the bride."

I only hear the words man and wife. It was the first time that I got to remove the veil from the woman that I just married. As I lifted the veil, a bright light entered the room. I was looking at the most beautiful human being alive. Her brightness makes the bulbs in the ceiling look pale. She was glowing. I was happy to give her my last name. I started to kiss her. I did not want to stop. This movie was too short. I want to play it repeatedly. I am sorry that it must have ended as one hundred people were watching us.

It is official. The cycle of love has taken a different turn. The wheels are rolling, and we are in line to create history together. This is beautiful. It is emotional. It is celebratory. The bridal party shepherd down the walkway. I held on to my wife tighter than before. Embracing the concept that two hearts join to beat as one.

We are no longer separated by ideology but joined by a common bond.

As we exited the church, the air outside was new. It was different. This looks like spring where the trees are green and fresh, and the blossoms are blooming. The bees were busy helping with pollination and collecting nectar to make honey. Birds appear friendlier than before. They are flying close and commingling with humans. Roses were used to create a pathway for us to walk. The smell was sensational.

It was refreshing to see the large sign on the limousine waiting to take us to the sunset. The sign marked "Just Married" was intended to remind everyone of the moment. A moment where God blessed our union. I watched Casey as she watched me. We could not believe that it finally happened. The festivity is fresh and there is no time now for reflection. The atmosphere is right for love, and we were embracing it.

Mrs. Casey Walker was glowing. The constant pleasantry forms a permanent smile on her face. She was eager to share her emotions with the people closest to her. I am by her side and commit to staying there forever. The grip they have on me is telling. It reminds me that I am her bodyguard. My new role is to provide everlasting security. I will build a foundation on solid ground. A building that is designed to store her heart. Strong enough to withstand any disaster.

The limousine left the church at the break of dawn. It was visible to see the sunset in the west. As we drive toward the sunset, it represents the closing of one chapter and the beginning of another. The bright orange sun was directing the car. This is a life compass that is guiding us to a new beginning. The sun was harmless. It was not hot. It was providing light to alleviate nature's problems. We're getting closer to the venue where the wedding reception is taking place. The sun was changing color. It was changing from orange to yellow. We noticed that it was going behind the mountain. Finally, it disappears. It left us, but we were not alone. The moon decided to take its place.

The royal couple reaches the hotel. I demand to stay with my wife. She assured me that she will be back shortly. Some of the ladies from the bridal party accompany her to the room where she changes her gown. She came back shortly and took her seat on the throne beside me. This was the celebratory phase, but it looks familiar. It is familiar because it takes the same form as my birthday party with the same speakers. Everyone showers us with praise and expresses their gratitude for our union.

This forum allows Casey to reflect on our new beginning. As a speechwriter and public speaker, she was not shy to express herself. Casey was long. She was concise and funny. Casey takes the opportunity to thank family and friends for their unwavering support of our journey. At one point, her voice was cracking. It was emotional and she was not afraid to show her feelings.

"We are human beings, real human beings with real emotions. We are not perfect, but our effort and understanding will develop perfection. Problems will arise, but it will be our effort that determines whether we solve them. We love each other and are committed to spending the rest of our lives together," Casey explained.

Casey cried opening. She was determined to complete her speech. I try to console her. I used my rag to dry her tears. I was careful not to disturb her makeup. She was strong. She was like a tree with several branches but developed roots to strengthen the structure. I see her as a delicate flower. A flower that is determined to grow under any condition. Battered by the winds and rain, but always grow new branches.

"Dan's family is now my family, and his friends are now my friends. We no longer have secrets, and we are committed to compromise. The wise words of Dan's mother will help to guide us in our quest. It is the power of compromise. On behalf of myself and my husband, we thank you all for coming, and for your support," Casey concluded.

It was well said. Casey speaks for both of us. I am proud of my wife. I am lucky to have a wife with such energy. Beauty and brain. I must show my appreciation. I looked around the room. Everybody was happy for us. It was a day that highlighted the love of a young couple. A couple who are determined to illustrate to the world the meaning of love.

There is a tradition at wedding receptions. It is a custom that I love. Anyone can use the utensil to knock the wine glass. Whenever that happened, I and my wife had to kiss. Tyler started the epistle. Periodically, several people join in the fun. We did not mind the game. It was fun to have two people who enjoy kissing each other and waste opportunities doing it.

We open the dance floor. After two songs everyone joins in. I could hardly dance to another song with my wife. She was moving around the room from women to men. Casey's father wanted the last dance. Even though I am the man of the moment, he deserves it. He gave me her hands in marriage. I am grateful. My mom was happy for me and demanded a dance. I couldn't take my eyes off my wife. I was like the Secret Service, monitoring the area to see where she was. My mother assured me that Casey would be fine. I looked at the time. It is getting late. We are expected to leave for the airport shortly. We are heading to Paris for our honeymoon. Far away from family and friends, but closer to Casey. We are ready for the journey.

CHAPTER 20

Marriage is a victory lap. It is the destination of a long race. We are celebrating and the place to highlight our love is Paris. As we journeyed on the ten-hour flight, Casey and I got an opportunity to reflect on the wedding. We were happy to form a perfect union. Destiny might be unknown, but we can dictate what will happen in the future. For now, we must concentrate on the trip. What are we going to do for the duration of the flight? We'd had little sleep in the last forty-eight hours, and we are determined to move forward.

The plane took off with the newlyweds in first class. Casey covers herself with a blanket and rests her head on my shoulders. I move her seat backward so she has enough space to stretch her legs. She positioned her face under my chin. Her mouth was less than an inch from mine. Controlling her breathing like a well-oiled machine with her minty breath breathing life into me. I poked her on the bridge of her nose with my index finger. Casey flinched. She moved her eyes in my direction and smiled. I could see her pupils warning me to stop. Every time the plane encountered rough weather; Casey would kiss me. The flight attendant would stare at us in admiration. The look on the flight attendant's face was puzzling. She was not uncomfortable. It appears that she felt that she was hindering our progress. I could tell that she wanted to say something. Finally, she looked up at us and smiled.

"I can see that you guys are in love. When did you meet?

You look good together," she disclosed.

Casey slightly tilts her head to the left to acknowledge the flight attendant, with her body hidden under the blanket.

"We just got married. We are on our way to Paris for our honeymoon," Casey replied.

The flight attendant screamed in amazement. Getting the attention of the other passengers. They did not know what was happening. Excess noise on flights these days might not be the best idea.

"Oh, Lord, that is so sweet. Congratulations."

She rushed to the phone and informed the pilots and other attendants of our status. Shortly after there was the sound of the "fastened seatbelt sign." The pilot announces that there were newlyweds on board.

"On behalf of One World Alliance and the entire flight crew, we want to congratulate you on your marriage. We are happy to have you flying with us today and we hope you enjoy your stay in Paris," the pilot announced.

Other passengers join in the fun. One by one they journey to our seats to congratulate us. Some people offer prayer, while others offer advice. They reiterate the gravity of love. The audacity that we take to achieve this milestone, and our tenacity to endure. We appreciate all the compliments and were humbled by the flight attendant. The fire is under control. The dust is settled, and the smoke is cleared. Exhaustion from the fumes was evident. It is time to rest. Casey yawned about three times. Her eyes were closing. She was fighting it, but sleep empowered her. I was watching over her. The crowd was friendly. No need for extra precautions, but I must do my duty. I swore to protect her until death does us part. I can do so much and no more. The vicious cycle of sleep is trying to attack again. It devours my wife and is hellbent on taking me down too. I will not go down without a fight. Then sleep pounced on me, and I punched back. My body is getting weak. I could smell defeat. Within seconds, sleep got the better of me. Casey was left exposed. No one was there to look after her. I was left at the mercy of the flight attendant, who placed a pillow under my head to support my neck.

I had a dream. I was having a great time in Paris when an angel approached me. She was dressed in red. That was suspicious to me. Angels are usually attired in white. She was beautiful. I thought it was Casey. The angel was upset when I mentioned Casey's name. She chastised me for not understanding the meaning of love. I was confused. We just got married. Shouldn't God be happy for us? Yet, this angel was having none of it. I try to convince the angel that I am in love with Casey, but she dismisses it as infatuation. She was annoyed. She was angry. The angel keeps walking up and down the same path. She was impatient. It was obvious that she was waiting on someone. I kept explaining myself. Every time I try to talk, she would place her hands on my mouth. Her hands were soft. I could smell the lotion on her hands. The angel was covering her face with a veil. I tried to see who it was, but she kept pushing my hands away. After an hour, she didn't want to hear from me anymore. She was walking away. I tried to follow her. She starts running. I chased after her. The angel was fading out of sight. I could see the beautiful red dress from a distance, as it disappeared. I called after her. She was gone.

I was talking in my sleep. I was not loud, but anyone close to me would hear the mumbling sound. My hands were gripping Casey tighter as if someone was taking her away. This is my honeymoon. I should be having a good time. I should be having good dreams, not nightmares. The angel in red tries to sow doubt about Casey. It was a method of division to confuse me. Casey is a sweet woman. She is the kindest woman I know. I will not be influenced by anyone. Even though I dismissed the angel as a nightmare, it haunts my subconsciousness. But I dismiss it as a spirit for evil. It is a fight against love. The spirit does not want to see love grow. She is determined to cut down every tree in my path. Wither and rot all branches and turn the barks in mulch. My head is underwater, but I am still breathing fine. The depth will not confine me. I will fight to keep my marriage. I was longing for love, and she found me. I was struggling and she rescued me. My duty to her is to ensure that she is happy.

The strange sound woke Casey. However, it was time to prepare our seats for landing. Paris welcomes us with open arms. We had so much activity planned. We left the hotel in a cab to the Wall of Love in Montmartre. There were thousands of names scribed on the wall. I took Casey's hands. I could see the joy in her eyes. She turned and hugged me closer. Her lips were trembling. No sound was coming from her mouth. Casey wanted to talk. It was magical. We started kissing. We were not alone, but our name was entrenched on the wall. Dan and Casey's names will remain in Paris forever. I just want to hold her in my arms. I did not want to let go. It felt like we were kissing for the first time. The environment causes her lips to taste better. There was little time for talking. The birds were understandable and friendly. Walking at our feet in unison as they celebrate their relationships. Love was in the air. The wind was blowing Casey's hair in the opposite direction. Trying to hide her face and impede our kiss. It was no match for us. Our hands were working like wiper blades on a car. Moving from left to right to fend off the breeze. This moment was made for television. The production crew should be here. This is a Kodak moment, and these memories will be cherished forever.

We strolled down the street where the trees were waving at us from both sides. The butterflies were flying in formation making heart shapes. I place my hands around Casey from behind while we walk down the street. Feeling the motions of her hips rotate while we strode. Before I could catch my breath, she started kissing me again. We could not move fast because we were caught in an awkward position. This is what love means. Helping each other along the way. Each tiny step means a moment together. We were gobbling up every romantic scene that Paris has to offer. We enjoy each other's company. There is not enough time in the days for us. We crave love and the love doctor attends to us, writing prescriptions to heal our wounds and mend our heartaches. We are lucky to have each other.

As night fell, we headed to the wine bar. Casey was eager to explore. The moment of reckoning is here. We were on top of the Eiffel Tower having champagne.

"This is the height of our love. God blessed us to view Paris from a vantage point. We are overlooking the world and the world is smiling at us," Casey proclaimed.

Her eyes were like marble. The lights from the chandelier were beaming like a laser. She loved the environment. Taking several deep breaths while she sips from the champagne glass. Observing every moment that passes by. She hums the song that was playing with pride. Shouting from the depth of her voice as if no one else was around. Casey has no care in the world. She was loving Paris and Paris was loving her back.

"I am happy to have you as my wife. Every minute that goes by, I love you more. Paris enhances your beauty and elevates my love for you."

"I feel so alive. This sky is the limit. Life is just for living and I am happy that I am enjoying the moment. Dan, my life was empty. Working seven days per week and missing out on the greater things in life. You give my life meaning. I am grateful for that."

"Casey, I look forward to spending the rest of my life with you. I was shy. I was reserved. But you bring out a different part of me. You make me brave. I am not afraid to express my love to you anywhere."

Casey looked at me and smiled. She extends her arms so I could pull her closer. She stands on one leg with her body pressing against mine, with her lips waiting to devour mine. Our kisses disturb the climate. Lightning and thunder could be heard from a distance. Rain started. The drops were getting bigger. People were scrambling for cover. Casey decided that she was not leaving.

"This is the beauty of nature. Let us enjoy it. Stay in it with me, Dan."

The rain was pounding us from head to toe. Casey's hair lay still across her face with water dripping down her body. Her clothes cling to her body with her physique visible. It was like taking a shower, but the water was coming from above. We played in the rain. Holding hands, kissing, and exploring the element. Casey was enjoying herself. She loves nature. We walked to the hotel. People admired our passion. It was romantic. We had the support of Paris.

Casey went into the bathroom to dry her hair. Her phone was ringing in her bag. I went to get it and realized it was from her job. Casey came out wrapped in a towel and asked me if I wanted to join her. I rushed into the bathroom to slip out of the wet clothes. The floor was wet from the water from Casey's clothes. I ripped my clothes off and rushed back into the room. By then, the phone was ringing again, and Casey answered it. She indicated that it was her boss and he wanted to discuss a new venture that the company was undertaking. They were on the phone for the next two hours. After the phone call ended, Casey came into the room. By then I had taken a shower and almost fallen asleep.

"Honey, I have bad news. The deal for the biggest venture at work will take place tomorrow and my boss has asked me to be there for the signing. This is a project that is very important to me. I have been working on it for almost a year," Casey said.

"If that is the case, I will support your decision," I suggested.

"We will be leaving on the first flight in the morning, so let us start packing," Casey points out.

I was disappointed. The honeymoon went so well. It was supposed to be three days. I must support my wife in her endeavor. We are a unit. After packing, it was late, and we went to bed. A long flight awaits us in the morning to California.

CHAPTER 21

Life tends to shortchange people. It forces us to accept what we can get until we get what we want. My honeymoon was cut short, but I am grateful for the time we spent together. I am heading back to North Carolina. For the first time, I will be blessing my home soil as a married man. I feel a sense of responsibility, honor, and purpose. My left hand feels different. There is a permanent fixture on my finger, and it can be seen from miles away. This visit will be special because I won't be long. I am moving to California to join my wife. I finished school and got a transfer from my job to work at the headquarters in California.

When I arrived in Charlotte, the people were happy to see me. It was like a party; the music was beating in my ears. Every stranger looks familiar. The airport looks different. I am like a famous movie star, and everyone wants to watch the show. I build self-confidence. Love is a beautiful thing. It was amazing that an introvert could be transformed into a sociable man. Even the road to my house looks different. My mind is playing tricks on me. It might be anxiety. I love North Carolina, but I am eager to move to California to live with my wife. Who could blame me? Love has molded me into a new being.

I tried to get into the house, but it was harder than usual. The door appeared to be glued to the hinges. It was heavy. It feels bigger than normal. I realize that the door inches needed to be oiled. They have not been open in a while. The house did not miss me, and the door did not want to let me in. It treated me like a stranger. It was so hard to open that I thought someone changed the locks. But I have no time to make new friends and no appetite to reconnect with old friends. I have found my lifetime partner. This is where my interest lie.

It was about one p.m. I decided to relax for a few hours. I lie in the room. Strange sounds were coming from every corner of the house. The sound was so loud that I thought that someone was repairing the house. The hammer was getting louder. I was afraid. It was the stillness of the house that was haunting me. I have not been alone for the past four weeks and the thought of loneliness aggravates my mind. The wind was making strange sounds. The fridge was trying to communicate with me. I was not interested. I am here to make final arrangements and in two days I will say goodbye. I moved from room to room trying to find comfort, but that was useless. I decided to go on the road to run some errands.

I am on my way to the office to clean out my locker and say farewell to my coworkers. This will be bittersweet as I have been working there for over ten years. We are like family. The bond is unbroken. I will miss Brandon the most. He was my big brother, teacher, adviser, and councilor. He was there for me in times of need, and I will never forget his kindness. As I drive inside the garage, a cloud of darkness covers the building. The lights were no match for the sadness that had unearthed our friendship. For the first time, there was no jubilation. Brandon or my boss did not meet me at the gate. No one was available to buzz me in. I use my access pass to let myself in. I had to swipe it more than three times for it to work. Even the access pass understands the gravity of the moment. People were working away as if I was nonexistent. Were they pretending to be busy to avoid me or was their workload too heavy? I could hear the spanner and the pliers talking to the cars.

I walked into the manager's office to collect my transfer, but he was on a call. He turned in my direction and raised his index finger in acknowledgment of my presence. He indicated that I should have a seat. While waiting, Brandon was passing the manager's office and saw me and stopped. He was surprised to see me. Maybe he thought that I had left for California. The look in his eyes was vague and he quickly looked away. His head turned to the passage and his body faced the office door. Brandon's body posture was saying something different from his facial expressions.

"Hey, Dan, are you here to ask for your job back? I am not giving up this promotion, but you can be my assistant," Brandon joked.

The atmosphere was strange. Brandon turns his back to me with his eyes fixated on the ceiling. This was like two young lovers dating for the first time. All signs of nervousness were evident, but they were determined to communicate.

"Oh no. I wish I did, but I came here to collect my transfer letter and to say goodbye," I responded. "I was coming to see you. I know you are busy in your new role and might not have any time to hang out later."

"We are going to miss you. You were the conscience of the garage, a good friend, and was a source of motivation. No one can replace you."

Brandon mustered the courage to face me, but his eyes were all over the room. He had been grooming me for this for a long time. Now I have found true love and am ready to spread my wings, he is not ready to let go. Brandon's actions can be compared to a dog chasing a car and once the car stops, the dog does not know what else to do. I am not worried about Brandon.

I know that he will find someone else to groom.

"Thank you for your kind words and I know you will step up to the plate. Congratulations on your promotion. You have the temperament to be a good leader and you will rise to the occasion. You guys will be just fine. I am now the Director of Operations in California, and I might just recruit you to be my assistant."

That statement caught the manager's attention. He pointed out to the person on the line that he will call him back. He made a sharp right turn in my direction and sprung to his feet.

"Recruit who? Did I hear right? One of my best workers is moving to California and you are trying to recruit the second in command. Are you trying to close this branch?" the manager inquired.

"I was joking. I was just telling Brandon how valuable he is to the team," I explained.

"OK. My job is to rebuild this team with Brandon as the supervisor, so I do not want you to put any wrong ideas in his head."

"Boss, you know that I am not going anywhere. I have your back," Brandon shouted. "Dan is married now so he does not need me anymore. Plus, he is well-behaved."

The manager patted him on the back and encouraged him to keep up the good work. Brandon worked close to me for years and everything that I knew I shared with him. His work attitude is different from his social personality. He might have a strange approach to love, but he is committed to his work. The manager indicated that he intended to train Brandon to take over from him. He handed me the letter and smiled. I could tell that he was pleased with my performance over the years.

"Eleven years ago, when you came here, you were just a kid afraid of the sound of the engine. You would flinch and cover your ears whenever we revved an engine. It was a big deal if grease caught your uniform. I am proud to see what you have become. Whenever a new vehicle comes into the garage, we will be proud to say that you help to design it. I am happy that I have had a hand in your development. You turn fear into hope and knowledge into opportunities. Please, promise me that you will not stop there. You will expand your knowledge to the highest level," the manager explained.

"You are my mentor, and I will reach out to you from time to time to get your opinion on several projects. But, for now, I just want to say that I am grateful for all that you have done for me. You employed me when I knew nothing and taught me everything. You tolerated me in my darkest hour. Thank you," I elaborated.

"I have to get back on this call, but I wish you all the best."

We walked out of the office and headed to Brandon's workstation. This is a separation, and the mood is tense. After ten years, I will be moving hundreds of miles away from my friends. I cannot live in two worlds and need to make new friends. But I hope to visit North Carolina often and keep in touch. The other employees were happy to see me and expressed sadness to see me go. Brandon was trying to stay busy, but I understand what he is going through. He is my best friend and we have been through good times and bad times. The atmosphere is sad, but it is for the better. As I said my final farewell and stepped through the main door, a feeling of loneliness came over me. It shows that I am missing something. My best friend didn't watch me go. We are hurt. He was affected and did not want to show his emotion. I will allow him to adapt to the environment and call him on my way to the airport.

Getting the uniform from my locker was sentimental. It was

greasy, displaying remnants of the oil from the engines. This was sad because I might not have had the opportunity to bathe in motor oil any more. It was a sense of achievement. The manager had this theory that the more oil and grease that is on the employees' uniforms, the harder he believes that they are working. It is like employing a painter with no paint on his clothes. He might be a professional, but you might not be comfortable employing him. I observe the garage as I leave. Things might appear the same now, but when I return, everything will be different. New faces seem to scare me, but I must familiarize myself with them. My surroundings will look new, but I must master the area. I am heading into a new role that requires the support of the entire staff. I am a new creation and a brand-new man. A natural being who believes that love can solve all problems. I embrace the theory that a happy man at home will be a happy man at work.

The memories of all my friends are fresh in my mind. It was like yesterday when Brandon was trying to find a woman for me. Dragging me all over town with him at parties and social gatherings. Introducing me to all his family members hoping that I make a connection with one. Even though he was not successful, he was determined to make a match. He never gives up on me.

It was like an hour ago when Tyler introduced me to online dating. When everyone else thought that it would not work, he encouraged me to stay the course. I owe him my life. He taught me what love is. He displays the beauty of two people enjoying each other's company. I am looking forward to attending his wedding.

Today is full of too many memories. It is not a day to cry, but a day to reflect on the past and use it to guide the future. This is a future that I am looking forward to. I am not a clairvoyant and will not pretend to be one. This means that I cannot see the future but am willing to find out what it has to offer. The mere mention of Casey's name makes me happy. I was longing for love. I question where it was. Now I have found it, I am eager to go back to California. This is the biggest decision of my life. I will be a stranger in and new land. But I am a big boy. I am grown. This decision can only make me stronger. I am determined to fight for life. I cannot do it alone. With Casey by my side, the sky is the limit.

CHAPTER 22

The days start zipping by and there is no resolution with Taylor. I need to tell her that I am moving to California. How will she react when I inform her? Should I tell her over the phone, or in person? These questions are nagging me. I decided to drive down to Greensboro and confront Taylor. She deserves my honesty.

I set out on my journey with a heavy heart. Knowing that there is no happy ending to my endeavor, I cannot in good conscience go away without telling her. I have one hour to plan my strategy. With the music blasting in my ears, I set sail to Taylor's house. It is calm seas, but it won't be for long. I cannot afford for this boat to overturn because I cannot swim. I know what time she gets home, and I intend to surprise her. Several scenarios keep flashing in my mind. What if she doesn't want to see me? What if she is not there, or what if she is fine with my actions?

I stopped and bought her a bunch of roses and a bar of chocolate. This dilemma is unpredictable. I drove up to her house. I need a moment to build courage. My heart is pounding in my chest. I sat in the car for a few minutes. The wedding band is still on my finger. I vowed to Casey that I would not take it off under any circumstances, and I intend to keep my word. As I walked up to the door, I looked to the heavens for support. My knees are shaking. I am losing my vision because everything in my sight appears blurred. Taylor's car is in the driveway. I walked up to the door. I paused. Should I come back tomorrow?

Should I call her from the car? I can't turn back now. I mustered the courage and rang the doorbell. My left hand was in my pocket. I didn't want Taylor to see the ring. At least, not at first. The door opened. It was like an earthquake. I whisper a quick prayer. My hope was for the earth to open and take me in. Taylor appears at the door. She was still in her work clothes. It was obvious that she was having dinner. There were remnants of chicken in her mouth and a drumstick in her hand.

"Hi, Dan, what a surprise. What are you doing here? You should call and tell me that you were coming here."

I was still searching for words. My actions must be quick. I do not have all night.

"I was in the area and decided that I would surprise you." I search for words.

"Who do you know in this area? You never come to Greensboro without calling me first. What is going on? I have not spoken to you in two weeks. Every time I call you it goes to voicemail."

"Are you going to invite me in? There is something I need to talk to you about and I believe that it is best to talk to you in person."

Taylor slid to the right and let me inside. I noticed the concern on her face. She locked the door and went back to the table to finish her dinner. I followed her to the living room. It was awkward. My left hand was still in my pocket and the flowers and chocolate were in my right. I handed her the gift hoping it would change her mood.

"Thank you, Dan, but I am still upset. I am used to your tricks. They won't work. You thought that if you called first, I would say no, so you just show up at my door."

"No, Taylor, that is not what happened. I have been trying to tell you something for the past two months. Every time I start you cut me off. I decided that you need to hear today. You needed to hear from me."

I got her attention. Taylor stops eating. She put the plate in the fridge, washed her hands, then walked back toward me. This time she stands over me. Her facial expression changed. I could tell she was trying to process what I was about to say.

"What is it that you couldn't tell me over the phone? You know me. You can talk to me about anything. I know you want a committed relationship, but I want to make sure that I am ready. I do not want to make any mistakes. Please understand. I need more time to process my feelings. Are you ready to move on?" Taylor asked.

This is going to be harder than I thought. Taylor has feelings for me. I stand up. Walked around the couch about three times.

"Dan, you are scaring me. What is going on? Is your family, OK?"

"I don't know where to start. This is harder than I thought. Please sit down so I can explain it to you," I suggested.

"Why is your left hand in your pocket from the moment you walked in? Did it get injured in an accident?" Taylor asked.

I took a deep breath. Look her in the eyes.

"From the day we met, I promised that I would be honest with you. I believe that honesty helps to build trust. Tomorrow I will be moving to California," I explained.

Taylor's face changed from concerned to sad. She stared at me in disbelief. I am hurting inside knowing that the worst part is yet to come.

"Why are you moving to California? There are great things in North Carolina and in time you will realize your dream. You are a selfish man. You think that I chase you away because I am not ready to commit to a relationship. Fine. Go, and I hope you never come back!" Taylor shouted.

Taylor was getting upset but for the wrong reason. The tension in the room was fever-pitched. I was sweating. Taylor moved to the end of the couch. Then, moved again to the far side of the room. Her eyes were focused through the window. I walked over to her, but she moved again. As she passed, I tried to hold her with my left hand and my ring became exposed.

"Please let me finish. I need to finish. You might hate me for the rest of your life, but I need to come clean. I got married to a woman in California. I have been trying to tell you for a long time. I never meant to hurt you," I explained calmly.

"What? What the shit are you talking about?" Taylor screamed.

Her features changed. Tears were flowing from her eyes while she continued to scream at me from the bottom of her lungs. Her voice was cracking. The words were muffled.

"It was my fault that I did not tell you sooner. There is no excuse and I understand if you hate me for that."

"How could you do this to me, Dan? I care for you. You were the last person I thought would hurt me. I never want to see you again"

"Please listen to me. Only my mother cares for me as you do. I have tried everything, and you pushed me away. I was convinced that you did not want a relationship."

This is the saddest moment in my life. I didn't want to hurt Taylor. She is a good woman. She ran over to me, and I stepped back. I did not know what she was up to. Taylor was crying and yelling. She starts hitting me in the chest with both hands. I know she was upset. I know she was hurt. I held on to her arms and tried to restrain her. She had extra power. I tumbled over. I got up quickly and held her from behind. Forcing both arms to her side. I just want her to calm down. I lift her and take her to the couch and ask her to sit down. As she complied. I went into the kitchen and got her a cup of water. I offered her the rag from my pocket so she could wipe her face. On the couch, she starts pouncing on me again. This time, she was getting weak. I hugged her and tried to console her. Taylor lye on my shoulders. Suddenly, she stopped crying. Then her arms dropped to my legs. She wasn't moving. I realized that she fainted. I checked and found a pulse. I lie her back on the couch, then call 911. I was hoping that nothing happened to her.

The paramedics arrived on the scene within ten minutes and revived her. Taylor was moving, but her eyes were still closed. They decided to take her to the hospital for further checks. I drove behind the ambulance. I blame myself for everything. How could I be so cruel as to place so much burden on her? I will not forgive myself if anything happens to her.

At the hospital, I gave them all the information about her. They thought I was her husband. I told them that I was her friend. After several tests, the doctor informed me that she fainted. She advised that Taylor is resting now, but she can go home in the morning. I sat in the room at Taylor's bedside. It was very quiet. She was breathing heavily. I was waiting for her to wake up. At about three a.m., I fell asleep in the chair.

In the morning, I awaken to someone watching over me. Taylor was sitting on the side of the bed watching me. I was happy to see her. I sprang to my feet. I wanted to hug her, but I didn't know the mood she was in. I put her in the hospital in the first place.

"Good morning. How are you feeling?" I inquired.

"I am feeling great. The doctor said I fainted. She said I can go home when I am ready. Thank you for helping me," Taylor replied.

"I was worried that something would happen to you. I could not forgive myself."

"It is not your fault. I should have been more understanding. I was not ready for a relationship but expected you to wait for me. That would not be fear to you. You are a good person. You stood by my bedside the entire time."

"I must ensure that you are fine. You would do the same for me."

The doctor entered the room and checked Taylor and informed me that I can take her home. Taylor looked at me and smiled. I know that smile and she is back. On our way home, we stopped to get breakfast. We joked about what happened. Sometimes things happen for a reason.

"Dan, I was going to throw you out of my house last night. I was so shocked that you got married. I wanted to hurt you, but I can't. I wanted to hate you, but I realized that I pushed you away. My heart convinced me that if you are mine, you will come back to me. I will leave it to chance and see what life brings."

"Coming here, I was worried that this might happen. I couldn't be so irresponsible as to tell you ever the phone. I know if I call you and inform you that I am coming, you will say no. I am done with tricks. I want to be honest with you."

"It is not like I can convince you not to get married. However, I want you to go to California and work hard to make your marriage work. Whatever I want for myself, I want for another woman."

"Thank you, Taylor, for being a friend. I will keep in touch."

Some events in life are hard to predict. People deserve to be treated with respect. Taylor has been good to me, and it pains my heart to see her suffer. I hope that she finds someone that will treat her like a queen. The time I spent in Greensboro will not be in vain. I found a good friend that will last. It is time to say goodbye and set on my journey.

CHAPTER 23

I am not ready to say goodbye to North Carolina. This is my home, but I am ready to embrace love wherever it is. My mother agrees. She is helping me to pack for my journey. I am being prepared for a life away from my house. It is amazing how fast the bugs and spiders realize that I am leaving. They moved in before I vacated the building. It will be in the care of my parents.

"What should I do with this house, Mom? I do not want to sell it. It is my first house and I want to leave it for my children."

"That's a good idea. I might rent it while you are gone. I cannot allow spiders to take over. Your father suggested that we rent it to one of our church members. We would open a college fund with the monthly payment."

"Will it be in my name?" I asked.

"No. I will keep it in my name until your kids reach sixteen. When are you planning to have a baby? Sooner than later, I hope."

"I don't know, Mom. Casey and I never talked about kids."

My mom turned and looked at me. You could see the anger in her eyes. She zipped up the suitcase and walked over to me. Her hands were positioned on her head.

"What! Do not tell me that you have been dating for more than two years and never talked about kids. What if Casey does not want kids? I need my grandbabies, you hear me."

"When the time is right, we will talk about kids. It does not change anything if Casey does not want kids. She is a professional and might not want to disrupt her career."

My mother is getting agitated. The more I talk the angrier she gets. I went over to her and placed my hands on her shoulder.

"I have a bad feeling about this, Daniel. My gut is telling me that something is wrong."

Whenever my mother calls me Daniel, I know that I am in trouble. I need to assure her that things will be fine. But how can I provide assurance when I don't know Casey's opinion on the topic?

"Drop it, Mom. I promise that I will talk to her as soon as I get to California."

"If you say so," Mother grumbled.

As she draws the boxes closer to her, my mother empties the ones that I put together and folds them over.

"Why are you emptying the boxes and packing them over?" I asked.

"Do you call this packing? The things were tossed in these boxes from a distance. The clothes should be neatly folded and placed at the bottom. Anything that can be easily broken should be placed in the middle. I will use clothes to separate them."

My mother scolds me for being tardy. I took my luggage downstairs because I knew that she was going to rearrange it. Nothing is better than my mother's touch. I did not want to challenge her because I want her to forget about me having kids. All the old stuff was placed in garbage bags. I took them outside so the garbage truck could pick them up. My mom took all my games, toys, and some of my clothes. She will donate them to a local charity.

"You are moving in with your wife and I cannot allow you to take this old stuff."

"Whatever you say, mom."

She strolls into the kitchen and picks up a bottle of water. I followed behind her. The issue with Taylor still bothers me and I want to get her thoughts on the matter.

"Mom, I want to talk to you about something. I am interested in your opinion."

"What is it?"

"Have you ever found yourself thinking about someone else while you are married to Dad?"

She looked up at me and smiled. She was glowing. It appears that she was back in her comfort zone. My mother took my hand and asked me to sit beside her.

"I think about different men all the time. That is natural. However, you need to understand that you are married and make a commitment to love one person until death." My mother elaborates, "Whatever you do, your wife and your family come first. "You should not do anything to jeopardize that."

"Do you remember Taylor?" I asked.

"How could I forget that sweet girl? Your father and I were hoping that you hit it off, but it was not meant to be."

"I find myself thinking about her. She was nice to me."

"I understand, but you are married to Casey now. You need to move on."

My mother releases my hands and starts dusting the furniture. I know that at this point she was finished with the discussion. She reinforces the family values that she taught us growing up. Mom starts humming a song. She is getting louder. It was a sign that I should stop bothering her. I get it. A mother should protect their children's marriage and try and eliminate all distractions. I will be leaving for California in a couple of hours. Why am I thinking about another woman? Why do things start to get complicated when they should be easy?

The sun is out in full strength, pushing any dark clouds in sight. Signaling the start of a new day in my life. It is the start of a lifetime with Casey. It will be great. It is a good feeling. The thought of waking up with a beautiful woman for the rest of my life. Who could ask for more? There are some lingering questions. Questions that are trivial but require answers anyway. What will I sleep in? Which side of the bed will I take? My mind is busy, but I am mentally ready. Ready to face the world of love. Anxious to capture the beast of doubt. Killing it would be ideal. But chasing it away will be acceptable. I am a warrior. Training for thirty years to understand the dynamics of love. I am equipped to challenge orthodoxy.

Mom packs several types of books in my luggage. She explains that reading will play a large part in my marriage. Reading will inform me about real-life experiences and keep me focused in trying times.

"I packed some romance novels, memoirs on relationships, science fiction, emotional challenges, and a Bible. This will help you to focus on positive aspects of life while helping you to understand the world around you," Mom stated.

I was puzzled. I thought to myself why I needed all this literature. Am I going to war in California? But, again, it is the role of parents to prepare their children for the challenges that will arise.

"What will I do with memoirs? I am anticipating a great life with Casey. We understand each other," I point it out.

My mother looks to the heavens for support. I could tell what she was thinking, God help him. She took a deep breath and turned to me like a teacher scolding the kids for not submitting the assignments.

"You might think that life is a straight line and is easy to identify the starting point and the finishing point. But life is more complex than you think. It is uncertain. The line is curvy. There will be times when a part of the line is erased, and you don't know where to turn. It is good to read memoirs to understand the life of those before you and how they maneuver the lines."

As I paid attention to my mother's lecture, I could hear the concerns in her voice. A mother fears that her son might not understand the basic function of love. I believe that love is a beautiful thing. Yes, it is. But I might not understand the rules of the game. It is a game that has many stages. A game that has many winners and losers. My mom just wants me to learn the game. Whatever the outcome, when the game finishes, will be acceptable to everyone involved.

"OK, Mom, I get it."

"I hope so. I did not raise a fool. You are a smart boy."

"You are a little harsh on me today, Mom. I thought you would be nicer to me on the day that I am leaving."

"It is not my job to be nice as a mother but to prepare you for the real world. It can be harsh out there. The world will chew you up and spit you out."

"I am glad that I have you to guide me."

"I will always be there for you."

As the world awaits the start of a new couple, I can be assured that I am ready. I am more prepared than the day before. I put the bags and boxes in my mom's car. I walked through the entire house for the last time. Talked to and explained to the empty house what happened. I am going to miss these walls. The nights might not be that quiet to allow me to hear the doors and windows talk. Their voices will be heard. Their opinions matter. The memories of this house will follow me to California. My mother is outside with the keys waiting to lock up. She realizes that I am having my moment. It is time to leave. Stillness came over me. Darkness could be seen through the house. I walk toward the front door. This doesn't feel like victory. My head is down. Sadness came over me. It feels like I am stealing away in the middle of the night. Being kidnapped by strange forces. No one is here to rescue me. I will try to escape.

My mother's car set sailing down the road. I keep watching the house through the rearview mirror. I can't let go. I can see my house from a distance. The image had disappeared. I am sad. I feel like crying. I am abandoning my state of birth for greener pastures. Am I ungrateful? Love does not think so. It promises me happiness on the other side of the flight. My mother remains quiet. She realizes that I am going through the motions and provides me with enough space to mourn.

At the airport, Mom chided me not to be a stranger and to visit often. She kisses me goodbye. This time was different. She knows that I will be on the other side of the country. No more weekend visits. Her last child has grown, taking the world by storm, and facing the world on his own. She is worried. Any parent should be. I will be in good hands. She thought of me well. It was time to fly. My wings are developed. The world is waiting, and I am ready to face it. We will cross paths again. It might not be every month, but I will continue to be in the frame. That famous picture frame hangs up in her house. One that tells the whole story. The story of love and survival. I will remain in contact.

CHAPTER 24

The sun is about to set in California, and it will have me in its forecast today. Far away from home is a boy from North Carolina determined to make his mark in the big city. The escalator was filled with passengers taking their own time marching to baggage claim. I cling to the right rail taking control of my space. Observing the people around me to see if Casey is anywhere in sight. I will need a large truck. I have two boxes, three suitcases, and a carry-on. I gather the luggage and place it in a corner of the lobby. Casey was nowhere to be found. After ten minutes, I call her. The phone went to voicemail for the first time. The second time it disconnects on the first ring. I was worried. I thought that maybe something was wrong. On the third try, Casey answered.

"Hi honey, where are you?" I asked.

"Shoosh! Are you at the airport already? Time got away from me. Casey responded.

"Yes, I am here in the lobby waiting on you."

"I am in a meeting and don't know what time it is going to finish. Can you hang on and let me see if I can leave early?"

Casey placed me on hold. I could not believe what I heard. This is my first night in a strange land and I am left on my own. I know Casey is busy, but the arrangements could be better. After thirty minutes, I hang it up. An hour went by, and I decided to call an Uber. I arrive at the house at about eight p.m. The house was dark. There was no one home. The driver could not stay so I put my stuff in the driveway. I did not remember the code for the alarm, so I decided not to try it. For a moment, I thought it was a dream. How could this be? I am stranded outside in the cold at the house that I am supposed to live in. I do not have a key and cannot remember the code. I was talking to myself. Moving up and down the driveway to keep warm. Suddenly, I saw a blue light flashing. It is heading in my direction. This car was getting closer. It was the police. Two officers flew from the vehicle and approached me.

"Good night, sir. We got a call from the neighbor that a strange man is standing in the driveway," one police officer explained.

"I am Casey's husband, Dan Walker. I just moved here from North Carolina. I don't have my key yet and I forgot the code to open the door."

"Can I see your ID?" The other officer asked.

I handed the officers my driver's license and went back to my bags. He went to run the license while the other officer kept his eyes on me. The experience is frightening. This was supposed to be a special night where the journey begins. It was not meant to be. I am about to be arrested. I inform the officer that the Ranger Rover in the driveway is mine and is registered to me. They ran the plate and realized that I was telling the truth. They believe that I am not an impostor.

"Do you have a number for Casey? We need to talk to her."

He dials the number and steps over to his car. I couldn't hear what he was saying, but he was on the phone for about five minutes. After the call ended, he stepped over to me.

"We want to apologize for the misunderstanding. After talking to Mrs. Walker, we confirm your story. We will stay here with you if you want until your wife lets you inside."

"Thank you, but I will be fine."

My status has been upgraded from a suspect to a stranded stranger. I am left believing that karma might be punishing me for something I did in the past. What could that be? I try to live up to my ideals from when I knew myself. As the officers drove off, Casey called.

"I am sorry that I got caught up at work and for the incident with the police. Are you OK?"

"Yes, I am fine. I need to get in so I can come out of this weather."

"The key is under the right tire of your truck/"

"When are you getting home?"

"I will be there in ten minutes. I will stop and pick up something to eat. Make yourself comfortable until I get there."

"I will. See you later."

I retrieve the key and open the door. Inside was like heaven's door. It was warm and comfortable. I pull the luggage inside to safety. I was saved by the bell. I was upset. I was hurting inside. Trying to identify the rational for Casey's action today. Once I hear her voice, my mood changes. I understand her life and the job she has. There will be days that her job takes precedence over mine. I knew what I was getting myself into and I am prepared to live with it. I sat on the couch. The pressure off my feet was like a miracle. I am a king on my throne. It felt special. Special because I was on my feet for hours. I stretch out my legs as far as they can reach. Lye on my back and stare into the ceiling. For a moment, I was back to reality. I was jittery. I was trembling. I was seconds away from being arrested and hauled to jail. It did not feel good. I did not have anyone to share this experience with. I will not tell my parents because they will be worried. But I need someone to talk to. My journey just started, and I am feeling lonely. It was not supposed to be. I should be greeted with open arms. I fantasized about this day. The day when I moved from North Carolina to join my wife in California. There would be a red carpet. A limousine was waiting for me at the airport. My wife waiting at baggage claim eager to love me. It was wishful thinking.

I am an optimist and refuse to believe that life will look like this. This is a one-off situation that will not recur. As I lie there thinking, the door opens. It was Casey. She entered the house and handed me the food. She sat at the other end of the couch. I noticed that she is dressed casually. Although she looked sexy, she was more showing skin than clothes.

"Are you going to greet me with a kiss? Get over here, honey," I insisted.

"We will have a lifetime to do that. I am sticky now and need to take a shower. I will help you to unpack as soon as I am finished."

Casey left to take a bath. I know strange things have happened to me in the past, but this is concerning. Casey pretends as if nothing happened today. She did not even want to know how my day went. I guess the evening is long and there is enough time to catch up. The smell of the food was escaping from the bag. It was trying to get my attention. The scent was calling my name and I responded. There was a popular saying from my mom that all food tastes good when you are hungry. But this was the best Italian food I have tasted. It melted in my mouth like water. There was nothing left for evidence.

Casey came out in pink lingerie that was just below her waist. There were perfect stitches highlighted at the helm with most of her back exposed. She was floating in thin air. I was searching for her wings. She was not walking. At that point, I realized what I have. The most beautiful woman in the world will be mine forever. She moves across the room to the walk-in closet, and I follow her like a pet. Her body was like a magnet, it was sucking me in. We spent several hours unpacking the clothes, but I was distracted. I couldn't take my eyes off her. I did not have enough shoes to make an impact on the shoe closet. Casey turns to me with a smirk on her face.

"We are going shopping tomorrow. I can see that you need some shoes. Also, you need to prepare for your new job on Monday," Casey claimed.

"I can start with what I have and increase my fleet as time goes by. It is better to take it one day at a time," I suggested.

"No, No. I will not allow this. My husband will not be searching for shoes. We will be going to the mall tomorrow."

"Sure, as you wish Casey."

Her dominance was concerning, but it shows that she cares. Sexy seems to come in all forms. If Casey demands a certain standard, it is my job to support her. I am a leader, but relationships demand compromise. I am new in a strange land. Nothing is wrong if Casey takes the lead. I convinced myself that I was doing the right thing.

"Babes, what side of the bed do you want? I heard that some people like to choose while others just lie on any available side?" Casey asked.

I laughed. I thought it was funny. It appears that Casey was reading my mind. This was one of the trivial questions that were plaguing my mind.

"Dan, what is so funny?"

"I was thinking about it today. It is a trivial issue, but I will take the right side. I am a protector and should be ready if any danger arises."

"Thank you, my knight in shining armor."

I put my phone on the bedside table marking my territory. I am the dominant force and expect that the tribe will follow my lead. She hands me a pack of rags, toothbrushes, and some soap. She organizes my side of the bathroom. It was set. I need to take a quick bath. I need to be ready for any attacks that might be anticipated. I am prepared for major warfare. This is the battlefield. Attacks should be coming from all sides. I want to be ready. I spend some time in the bathroom getting my act together. I want to seal the deal with my body spray. It will make me irresistible.

I put on a pair of shorts and a thin undershirt. Being deliberate allows my masculine physique to be on display. I want to make a grand appearance. To woo my prey. Attacking her where she was most vulnerable. Seizing on the moment where our sexual tension is at its highest. I entered the bedroom like a contestant performing on *America's Got Talent*. Waiting for Casey to give the command for me to take her. The room was quiet. Too quiet for comfort. Casey was sound asleep. The movie was canceled. The stars did not show up. My expectations were not realized. My dreams were shattered.

Casey's motionless body lies on the bed journeying through her second dream and leaving me behind. This was a day for the history books. Nothing seems to go right. A celebration turns into sadness. Bringing back the strange thoughts in my head. Anxious to see where it leads. I admire Martin Luther King, but I do not want to have a dream. I would rather live where the warmth of love is evident. Where the comfort of my bedroom represents the sanctity of love. Where relationships and marriage focus on happiness and prosperity. If reality is not in my grasp then I will take the dream. One that avenges the enemy of loneliness and promotes companionship. A dream that elevates romance that will create moments that can be cherished forever.

CHAPTER 25

Today is Saturday. I may not have gotten a hero's welcome yesterday, but I woke up in a new environment. An environment where my wife is next to me. Eliminating the threat of loneliness and promoting love. I am no longer held ransom for the beast that tormented me for years. It was conquered. I killed it. Victory is mine and it felt good.

The sun was up. Fighting its way through the drapes and blinds to greet me. It wanted to let its presence be felt. It was effective. It woke me up. I was lying on my belly and Casey's foot was tossed across me. My angel was resting with no care in the world. Her head rested on my chest and her right arm held me tight. It appears that she was conscious in her sleep. Clutching me in a stationary position where I could not escape. This is where I belong. In the arms of my queen. I did not want to wake her. I lie still with my eyes focusing on the ceiling. Watching the air from the air conditioner circulating through the room being attacked by the heat, it fights to stay relevant.

I could hear the birds outside bellowing my name. From a distance was the friendly woodpecker making his rounds as it caters to its young. It was busy for them on the outside but quiet for us on the inside. I heard a knocking on the bedroom door. The sound was coming from the floor. It appears that someone was kneeling. I could see a tiny shadow under the door. The knocking gets louder. I did not know who it was, so I remained quiet. Casey turned to the door.

"Go back to bed, Pepper," Casey shouted.

"Épée e mem," the dog responded.

I would hear the disappointment in the dog's voice. He was obedient. I could hear the ting steps making their way back down the stairs. He wants to see my wife with me. Luckily, Casey would have none of it. Casey curled back into my arms. She is at my mercy. Taming the king of the jungle. The lion wanted to roar. Should I attack my prey? I kissed the neck of my prey. Like a zombie, I want blood. Casey started screaming. Not for help, but to encourage the attack. The lioness understands the signal of her mate. I was the attacker, but I was getting weak. It appeared that the blood was leaving my body. This was a welcome party. I love music. We dance to every song. Who turns the radio off? I was energized yet confused. I could not tell night from day. California is on my mind. I fell asleep.

I had a dream. It was Sunday and we were late for church. We rushed outside and drove away. The church was full. There were several familiar faces. We sat in the back. The pastor recognized us and invited us to sit in the front seat. He informs us that we can take our son with us. I looked at Casey and she looked back at me. We realize that we forgot our baby at home. We rushed out of the church. I could hear the pastor's voice echoing throughout the church telling us to come back. I jump out of my sleep. The knocking was at the bedroom door again. This time, I open the door.

Pepper was happy to see me. He sprang into my arms. Making different friendly sounds. He was communicating with me. It was as if he wanted to know why we left him in my dream in church. Casey did not allow Pepper in the bed. The dog is smart. He was in my hands and I was walking toward the bed. He jumped out of my hands and ran over to Casey and started barking. It was his way of saying morning. He lye at the bedside waiting for Casey to acknowledge him. Casey rubbed his head, and he turned over on his back. He was happy to be greeted by his mistress.

I put on my robe and went downstairs to get a cup of coffee. My surroundings are new, but I am the man in the house now. I want to show that I am in charge. Like a fashion show, I parade the entire house in my robe.

"Honey, do you care for a cup of coffee? I am going to prepare a cup for myself," I beckoned Casey.

"Yes, dear. Please bring an orange for me," Casey replied.

There is a cost to happiness. I want to do more. The aim is to impress Casey. I peel the pineapple and cut it up into small pieces. Then washed some grapes, an apple, and a banana. I am making a fruit breakfast. I place them on the plate horizontally with the grapes in the middle. I put it on a tray and marshal the hallway like a waiter. I could see the look on Casey's face when I entered the room.

"Wow, you went all out for me. That's impressive. I know I was right when I married you."

"Anything for my wife. This is just the beginning of things to come."

"Are you trying to bribe me for my actions this morning? If yes, it is working"

"I am not trying to bribe you, but your kindness this morning was a motivating factor."

Even though her plate was full, I fed her with a slice of pineapple from my plate. Casey sat up on the bed enjoying my hospitality. She places a grape in her mouth and the bird feeds me. I was getting greedy, and she was in the mood to feed the needy. Casey fed me with more. It was a special moment. A moment to cherish. We understand each other more than we think. It was strange. Casey's phone did not ring all morning. I guess work was giving her a break. I appreciate it.

On our way to the mall, I observe Casey turning on her cell phone. I was shocked. However, I did not comment. I knew there was a reason for it. Everyone needs some special time without distraction. I did not think anything of it. Casey was acting as my tour guide. Showing me all the major landmarks and popular attractions.

"You need to pay attention, Dan. The next time you come here, you will be on your own. Some of the best restaurants, bars, clubs, and stores are here in the city. You should be able to find your way around easily."

"I will have you as my tour guide for the rest of my life. There might not be an urgent need to learn these."

"You will have me, but I am a busy woman. There will be a time when I will not be available. Remember that I spend a lot of time at work. I want to ensure that you can go out and enjoy yourself without getting lost."

"You have a good point, Casey. Brandon might be in town in a couple of months, and I need to know some hotspots where I can take him."

I realize that my status as a stranger will be over soon. It will require me to adapt to my surroundings as quickly as possible. I am prepared for the world and the world is ready for me. I am not a stranger to large cities, and I will survive. We stopped at several stores. Casey was on a shopping spree. We buy more clothes and shoes that will last me for a lifetime. My truck looked like I was going to goodwill to make donations. I appreciate the treat, but this was overkill. Casey changes my entire wardrobe. Buying most of the things that she likes without consulting me. I am just around for the ride. She was changing my appearance without asking me. Maybe this is what is accepted in the suburbs of California. I was concerned about this approach. However, my intentions are not to embarrass Casey around her friends.

The confirmation came when she took me to the barber. It was like taking her ten-year-old son. I like it when my hair is high and puffy. Casey instructed the barber to cut it off. I could not believe what I was hearing. I turned and looked at her. My eyes were wide open. She could see the descent on my face, but she didn't retreat. I did not want to create a scene in the barber show. How could I stay silent? My hair was my strength. She removed my crown. I was muted. On my way home, I did not speak. Once I reach home, I muster the courage to confront her.

"Casey, what was that about? I thought we were a team. You did not consult me on any. You speak for both of us."

"Dan, I have lived in California all my life. A lot of people know me. I do not want to be embarrassed. Please work with me here."

"Are you ashamed of me? I thought you loved me for who I am. But it is obvious that you are trying to create me in your image."

"Don't say that Dan. All I did was enhance your appearance. You look sexier, classier, and approachable."

"You are missing the point. I do not have a problem with change. I welcome change. However, I am an adult. You should consult me. I should have a say in how I dress or how I cut my hair."

"Honey, you are blowing things out of proportion. The next time, I will let you decide everything."

Casey smiled and walked away. It was obvious that she would have her way. I cannot even recognize myself. Maybe it was for the better. This was our first fight. It was not worth it. I need to apologize to Casey for all that she did for me. I went into the bedroom to talk to her and noticed that she was on the phone. She beckoned to me that it was her boss. I went back downstairs to the TV room. I started watching a movie. It started an hour ago, but I did not care. I just want to watch something to put my mind at ease. I heard a message coming through my cell phone. It was Taylor.

"Hi, Casey's husband, how are you? I just came in and my mind ran on you and decided to check up on you."

"I am OK. Not as good as I hoped, but it is early days. There will be time for improvements."

"Did something happen? You know that you can talk to me about anything. Our friendship doesn't change," Taylor explained.

"It is nothing really. Just some disagreements. It will work itself out," I responded.

"Good. Dan, please spend time with your wife. Show her that she is special. Make her feel appreciated."

"I will."

I am happy to talk to Taylor. I need someone to talk to, but I am not sure that Taylor is the right person to talk to about my wife. I sat in the TV room for about three hours reflecting on my life. Maybe Casey was right. I am blowing things out of proportion. I didn't want to go to bed upset. As Casey finished her call, I sat on the bed beside her. She was expecting confrontation, but I was there to make peace. It was about compromise. Everything she did for me was in the interest of love. We cuddled together and fell asleep.

CHAPTER 26

The first three months of living in California are complicated. It was filled with mixed reactions. I was convinced that things would get better. Maybe I was wrong. I got married because I craved someone to spend the rest of my life with. I was hungry for companionship. Maybe I was mistaken. The forces of life have not been kind to me. I need a redo. It is not so easy.

I am at home alone most of the time. Casey is consumed with work that takes her away for days at a time. It was our first anniversary and I wanted to surprise Casey with a bunch of flowers and a lunch date. I turned up at her job unannounced. In the lobby, I introduced myself and informed the receptionist that it was our anniversary and I wanted to surprise Casey with flowers. As I mention my name, the receptionist looks up at me with a smirk on her face. As if she wasn't sure who Dan Walker was, she looked at me again.

"Mr. Walker, that might not be a good idea to surprise your wife. I am afraid I will be forced to inform her of your presence."

"Why not? If she is in a meeting, I will wait. Please do not spoil this day for me. This is the least I can do for my wife. Do not deprive me of that moment."

"Give me a moment, sir, let me talk to my boss and get her advice on the matter."

I stood to the side while she consulted with her boss. Within a minute, the manager was at the front desk talking to the receptionist. They were whispering, I could not hear what they were saying. She then beckoned to me, and I walked back toward her.

"So, you are Casey's husband," the manager asked in a mocking tone. "I don't believe that she is here, but I will let her know that you stopped by."

"But the receptionist just told me five minutes ago that she was here. What is going on? Can I see her?"

"The receptionist was mistaken. Casey is not in her office. She left earlier for a meeting downtown. You can leave the flowers and I will make sure that she gets them."

I handed the flowers to her with a note and thanked her for her time. As I turned my back to walk, I could hear a giggling sound. I quickly turned around and saw the ladies laughing at me.

"What is so funny? Do you care to share?" I asked.

"We are not laughing at you, sir," they responded in unison.

"But I just caught you looking at me and laughing. Have my eyes deceived me? Am I lying?"

"We are just happy to meet you. Casey talks so much about you, so it was an honor when I heard that you were here," the manager explains.

I did not buy their explanation, but I decided that I would not challenge it either. I walk through the door without looking back. I find myself talking to myself. Asking myself outstanding questions. Something is wrong, but I do not know what it is. I called Casey twice from the car and she does not answer. I went back to work. My office is on the first floor, close to the production plant. We were working on a new model that was expected to be released in one month. I want to clear my head. The event today was bothering me. I step into the plant. The machines were busy retrofitting new cars. Employees were focused on the task at hand and hardly noticed me. It is refreshing to observe a vehicle being built from scratch. I tend to participate in the process when I need someone to talk to.

On my way home, Casey called. She ignored my calls all day. Today is a special day and I thought it meant something to her.

"Hi, Dan, I got your flowers today. I was in a meeting all day and could not break to come to see you."

"But they told me that you were out of the office attending a meeting."

"They did not want to disturb me. They know how intense these meetings can be and no one wants to be blamed for losing the company a major client."

"What time are you coming home? Today is our anniversary and I made a reservation for us at The French Laundry at nine p.m."

"That might not be a good idea. We are meeting with an important client tonight. This is one of our largest accounts and we need to secure the contract. It might take us all night."

I couldn't believe what I was hearing. This is like a fairytale. No one could make this stuff up. Married life cannot be this complicated. I have not blessed my eyes on my wife in months. Casey comes home late at night and before I could acknowledge her, she is fast asleep.

"I guess we can celebrate another day. I will cancel the reservation and order something for myself."

"Dan, the most important thing is that we have each other. No anniversary can define us. We are defined by our commitment to each other. I must go, but I will try and call you later if I get a chance."

Before I could respond, Casey hung up. I pinched myself. I want to make sure that I was not dreaming. Spending a special day by myself taking deliveries. I was lonely. Lonelier than when I was single. When I was single, I did not expect any company. I was not disappointed. Now I am married, I spend more time alone than at any other time in my life. How long can I take this? There must be a point where our relationship takes precedence over Casey's job. I have an important job, but I do not live at work.

Time is moving fast. I curled up on the couch. I rented a movie. The movie was about a man living with his wife for twenty years. After being captured by the enemy, his wife thought he died and started dating. One day she came home and saw that her husband was alive. She tries to break off the relationship and reunite with her husband. The hardest challenge was to get the husband to trust her again. The movie ends at about two a.m. I check my phone as I might have missed a call or a text from Casey. Nothing was there.

Casey did not come home that night. At least she should send me a message, so I know that she was fine. I think she is taking me for granted. I am dying inside. I need someone to talk to. I could not sleep. I toss and turn all night. My head was hurting. It appears that I was losing my mind. My chain of thought was broken. This is the first time that I felt like screaming from the bottom of my lungs. I took a Panadol, drank a bottle of water, and fell asleep.

I reach work late the next day. Being distracted and confused, I called Taylor. I needed someone to talk to. I shared everything that happened to me from the first day I arrived in California to the present. Taylor was guarded in the advice that she gave me. She didn't want to discourage me from my relationship, but she was concerned about what was happening. Taylor agreed with me that what was going on was not normal.

"Something is missing from the puzzle, and I cannot seem

to figure out what is," I lamented.

"I am not insinuating anything. But do you think that she is having an affair?" Taylor asked.

"I don't know, but the incident at the workplace makes me think that something was happening at work. I was the laughingstock there. I need to confront her."

"No, that is not a good idea. I am a woman and I know how I would react if my husband accused me of an extramarital affair without evidence."

"So, what should I do? I have not seen my wife in forty-eight hours. I want to tell my mother what is going on. I hesitated, but at some point, she needs to know."

"Casey might be spending time at work. The optics are bad, but I want you to have a discussion with her and see where it leads."

"Taylor, you are always there for me when I need you. You are special. Any other woman would not take my call after how I treated you."

"You are special to me, Dan. I will always be your friend. You almost killed me, but you also save my life," Taylor joked.

"I am a changed man. I wear glasses now, so I hope that I am a better person. Hearing your voice helps me to relax and refocus. I can get things done now."

"Go back to work and I will check in with you later."

It was the call I needed. I am glad that I could reach out to Taylor and get her advice on my marital problems. I plan to observe Casey's actions in the coming month and if there are no changes, I have no other choice but to confront her.

After work, I stopped at a sports bar with some coworkers to play pool. I felt uneasy. They have been inviting me for months and I always decline the offer. It was good therapy to take out my frustration on the pool table. It was my best game. I was playing like a professional. Finding a target for my wrath and pounding the balls in the hole at sixty miles per hour. It feels good winning. It feels good getting some attention. Making my own decision and using my initiative. I need to make this a weekly event. Maybe a daily event.

I arrive home at about nine p.m. hoping to see Casey in the house. But it was not meant to be. It was another night. Repeating the same process repeatedly. Eating takeouts and watching television by myself. The house is my only friend. I spend more time with Pepper than I do with my wife. The dog is now my best friend. He is the only one I see when I get home. At least someone appreciates me. He is great with love and treats me with respect.

At the stroke of midnight, Casey arrives. I have not seen her in almost three days. As usual, I expect an expensive gift because she believes that it can mend all fences. It was a conscious guess. Your guess was as good as mine. She strolls across the far side of the TV room. Sitting heavy and weary, as if the world was on her shoulders.

"I am so tired. I need some rest. We have been at this account for three days and we finally reach an agreement."

"I am happy to know."

"You sound cold. Are you happy to see me? It doesn't appear so," Casey asked.

Before I could answer she stumbled toward the bathroom. Doing her routine, taking a bath, and heading to bed.

"There is something on the table for you," Casey shouted from the bathroom.

This is the first time I was not interested. My life is converted into a token. There is no need for human interaction. An expensive gift will do the trick. I need to grow up. I need to learn how to stand up for myself and defend my principles. How long will I be taken for a fool? I deserve better. I demand better.

CHAPTER 27

I am in the dark again. Trying to decipher what is wrong with our marriage. Am I doing something wrong? Contending with a wife that comes home every other day. On the phone at all hours of the night and claims that she is working. I need to grow a spine. I need to confront Casey and demand that she changes in the interest of the marriage. She never cooks for me. We have not gone out together in two years.

As I came in from work, there was a still in the house. I am longing for a good conversation. Feeling the urge to hold my wife in my arms and make love to her. I stroll into the bedroom. Running my hands along the line of the sheet on Casey's side. Trying to remember what it was like to see her on the bed. I could only smell the disinfectant that the cleaner used in the room. The smell of Casey's perfume was missing. This room does not remember her any more. I lie across the bed wondering what my next move is. I am uneasy. I lean against the wall with my hands on my head. Slowly, I sat on the floor with my back resting on the wall and my feet stretched forward. Trying to understand how I got here and why. I want to cry, but I must stay strong. My temper is boiling. My heart was beating fast. I am getting angry. Angry at the empty house. Angry at my existence. I called Casey and she did not answer. I left a message. The message was forthright. It was angry. It represents the moment. I expressed how I feel and demand that we must talk tonight. I did not know if she would respond, but something must be done.

Within an hour Casey's car drove into the garage. I barely recognize the sound. The sensor light outside did not come on. I suspect that the sensor did not even recognize her. Casey has not been at home before midnight in months. She came in and tossed her handbag on the floor. Visibly upset, she went into the bedroom and slammed the door. She grumbled under her breath going through the door.

"I did not sign up for this. My life was perfect before you got here. Now you are trying to control me. I will not stand for it."

I am still shaking. I need to control my temper. Something inside me told me to calm down. I walked into the kitchen and got a bottle of water. I drank half of it. Casey came into the kitchen.

"Why did you leave this angry message on the phone?"

"At least it got your attention. We need to talk, and it cannot wait. Sit down for a moment."

"I'd rather stand," Casey shouted.

My features start changing. I looked at her in disgust. "Sit down please."

I elevated my voice. Casey must understand that it is not business as usual. Tonight, I demand to be heard. She is taking me for granted. Casey is taking advantage of me because she feels empowered. She deposits the personality of someone who believed that she was superior and everyone else was beneath her. Casey realizes that tonight I am no pushover. She sat down and crossed her legs. Her face was positioned to the sky and her eyes looked elsewhere. It appears that I am not worthy of her time.

"What do you want? I am listening," Casey asked in a condescending tone.

"I don't know what is going on, but I want to find out tonight. I have not seen or touched my wife in months and that must change."

"You know I have an important position at work. My work is my life, and you knew that before you met me."

"Yes, I know that you work hard, but it is strange for you to live twenty minutes from work and not come home for three days."

"But, Dan, you know where I am. Why are you tripping?"

"I do not know where you are, and I know that you are lying."

Casey jumped up from the seat and rushed over to me and started yelling in my face.

"What, what do you mean? Are you calling me a liar?"

"Yes, you are lying."

Casey stormed into the bedroom and slammed the door. In seconds, she came back out cursing and swearing. Accusing me of disrespecting her.

"After you did not come home Monday night, I felt guilty. I thought it was the argument that we had the day before that you were upset about. You told me that you had meetings all night in the boardroom. I went there to make it up to you. I reached there at six p.m. and you were driving out. I stayed there for an hour to see if you would come back, and you didn't return. To be certain, I asked the security guard for you, and she said that you left for the day. He explained that he was certain because you log out. To compound the issue, he explains that there was no meeting scheduled for the entire week."

For five minutes there was absolute silence. I could see all the physical features of Casey's face transformed. She was shaking. Scratching her head. Her brain was working overtime to figure out something to say. Finally, the silence was broken. Casey was no longer upset. It was the calmest I have ever seen her since we got married.

"I was at my parents' house. I just think that it was important to tell you."

I know she was lying because her mother called the house and was asking for her. She even takes the dog for a couple of days.

"Casey, you need to communicate with me. We got married because we committed to keeping each other company. You have not been here for months. That needs to stop."

"I got caught up in my work and did not realize what was happening. I promise to do better."

Our marriage problems were not resolved, but this is a start in the right direction. I know Casey might not change. She realized that I knew that she was lying so she retreated. She sat in the chair like a toddler using her toes to scratch the carpet, wanting to retreat to a corner but did not know how to move. Her conscience was bothering her. I do not have any evidence that she was having an affair with another man, but there was no rational explanation for her actions. She was disconnected from the world. Casey does not know what was going on at home.

"I want to inform you that Brandon is coming to California for the weekend, and he will be staying here."

"Why?"

"Because he is my best friend and I have not seen him in a year."

"I do not think that it is a good idea. You do not see me carrying my friends here. Why do you think it is OK to invite your friends into my house?"

"I did not know it would bother you. I will tell him to stay in a hotel."

"Do not tell him about our life. I do not want our business to be all over North Carolina."

At that moment I realized what was happening. All this time Casey has asked me not to visit North Carolina, it was for a reason. She wants to keep me in California because she was afraid that I would tell my parents about her abuse. It worked. I have not seen my parents in two years. When they called, I kept the discussion short.

Casey's phone had rung several times in her bag. She keeps looking at me. She wanted to answer it. Her eyes were all over the room and it made her uneasy. I could tell that someone special was on the other side. Casey scratches her palm and gazes at the bag. The pressure was mounting. I went into the bathroom and turned on the tap. I could see Casey rushing to answer the phone. She was whispering. I could not hear what she was saying. I flushed the toilet and watched her place the phone back in her bag and sat back down. At that point, I realize that I am no longer the number one person in Casey's life. She might be discreet tonight, but I know that her true color will emerge tomorrow. I took too long to question her actions. I accept too many outlandish excuses. It might be too late to salvage the marriage.

The next day I went to the airport to pick up Brandon. I told Casey that we will be staying at a nearby hotel, but we will be at the house during the daytime. I am not a betting man, but I know she would use the opportunity to stay away. So, I gamble. I took Brandon home. We had a lot to catch up on. I will not sugarcoat what was happening to me. I will tell him everything. Once we reached the house, Brandon kept talking.

"Where is Casey? I have not seen her in a long time. I can see she got you hooked. You abandoned North Carolina."

I pretend not to hear what he says. I offered him a beer hoping to change the subject. But he keeps pounding me.

"Stop ignoring me, man. You are a big shot now. You have no obligation to answer me."

"Brandon, life is not what it seems. I came to California believing that I would be happy. It is my job to keep myself sane. My life is miserable."

"How could that be? You have a great job and a beautiful wife. You have everything that you always wanted."

My heart sank when I heard that. It hurt me because it is true. Those were my hopes and dreams for years. I was a smart man and allow material things to overpower me. Casey was right. She knows exactly what she is doing. I love material things and believe that kindness is love. If the gifts keep coming, I will not leave.

"You will be here for the next three days, so you will experience first-hand what I am talking about. Sometimes, Casey stays out for three days."

"What? Stays where?" Brandon asked.

"I don't know but I suspect where. But tonight is not about my troubles. I have a guest to entertain. We are hitting the club."

For the next few hours, I put my marital problems aside. Brandon and I party like it was the last day. Singing popular songs and dancing to every music. He put a smile on my face. The gray hairs that were appearing on my head disappeared. I was in musical heaven. Flocked by angels having innocent fun. I did not want the night to end. Tomorrow will be a new day and we promise to repeat the same process.

CHAPTER 28

The next morning was normal for me. Waking up to an empty bed, reminding myself that Casey is missing. Should I call 911? That is not necessary because she always shows up on her own in a day or two. My only fear is that Brandon is here to witness it. I will face humiliation. This time I will face humiliation with my head up. I am down but not out. I will rise again. I will rise stronger than before.

I went to check on Brandon, but he is still sleeping, soaking in the fun and excitement from the night before, and trying to master the moves and attitudes of the women from California. This is his chapter of the movie. Starring in a film where the lust of the world came crashing at his feet. It might be time to grow up someday. A day when he faces the challenge of a real relationship. I might not be able to lecture him about that, but the world will be kind to me someday.

I went to IHOP to get some breakfast. The heat was melting the plastic bag. My nose collides with the smell that energizes my sense of taste. I start driving faster. I fear that this smell might tempt me to start eating. As I entered the house, I could hear movements in the guest room. I went to investigate and discover that the king was awake. Looking through the window and admiring the backyard.

"At last, we have you back. I was a little worried that you would never wake up," I suggested jokingly.

Brandon turned and looked at me. His eyes were half closed.

Stretching his entire body to try to recover his energy. Brandon could hardly move. He was moving in slow motion. He was hurt. Hurt from last night's activities. Limping from a night of endless fun.

"What's up? Nice house you have here. I could stay here for another week if you want," Brandon replied.

That would be great. I would have someone to talk to when I get home from work, but I know that was not possible.

"That would be nice, but I have a lot of stuff to do this week. Maybe another time I will invite you down for the entire week. Come and have breakfast before it gets cold."

We headed into the kitchen. The mood was tense. It was obvious that something was on Brandon's mind. He was roaming up and down the kitchen with the food in his hand. Looking in the hallway every time he heard a sound. Glancing at me for answers.

"Will Casey join us for breakfast?" He finally musters the courage to ask.

"She is not here."

"Oh! Where is she?"

The lines on his forehead were visible. He was concerned. These are legitimate questions, but I do not have the answers. Should I tell him a lie to save face?

"I honestly don't know."

"Are you for real? You told me last night, but I thought that you were exaggerating. This is not good."

There was a long pause. I did not have an answer for him. My voice was cracking from inside, but I must remain strong. My life had caught up with me. I must come out of the shadows. The facade of living a happy life must end. I will confront my shadow. I cannot be afraid of it.

"I am reassessing my options. I need a break from this place to clear my head."

"Why not come back to North Carolina for a week to see if the situation will improve? Anything is better than nothing."

"I will think about it and let you know by the end of the month."

Brandon was not convinced. I could see the look on his face, but he wanted to show compassion. I was in a bind and needed his pity. The next two days were wild. We visit every attraction, nightclub, and sports bar in California. Every good thing must come to an end. It is time for Brandon to get back to North Carolina. I dropped him off and the airport and headed to work. I was more relaxed than the week before. Brandon gave me a reason to put aside my problems and see life for what it was.

That evening, I left work at about eight. I was re-energized to clear some outstanding tasks. Casey's car was in the driveway. As I open the door, all that energy dissipates. She meets me at the door and tries to kiss me on the lips. I turned my head away and her lips pressed again my jaw. Casey wrapped her arms around me, and I pulled away. I was not in the mood for another fight.

"What is your problem? I am here alone for the entire weekend, and this is the greeting I get," Casey utters.

At that point, I thought I was dreaming. I need to wake myself up. I could not believe what I heard. Casey was lying to my face. Not just lying. She was lying with impunity. I walked into the bedroom, and she followed me there. I lie on the bed and draw the pillow over my head. My mind was in a different place. I just want to hide from the world. Casey dragged the pillow off my head and tossed it on the floor. In a rage, she kicked it across the room.

"Look, I am not in the mood to fight tonight. I just want to be alone for a minute," I suggested.

"I will not be ignored. You are being childish. I am talking to you, and you keep walking away. You complain about my actions, and when I try to do better, you push me away."

I want to tell her that I was at the house for the entire weekend, but I decided to play the fool. My temper was at boiling point. I need some fresh air. I went into the TV room and turned the channel to MSNBC news. This is a way to relax and understand the topic of the day. After an hour, I fell asleep. When I woke up, it was time to prepare for work. Casey had already left.

On my way to work, I called my mother. This was long overdue. There was a time when I could discuss anything with her. Casey convinces me to delete them from our lives. She said it would be better for us to work out our problems.

"Hi, Mom, I want to talk to you about me and Casey. I have not been totally honest with you."

My mother was getting excited. She was screaming on the phone. Maybe she had something else in mind.

"That's OK, son. Tell me the good news. Please tell me that Casey is pregnant."

"No, Mom, I am sorry. Casey does not want kids. I mentioned it to her last year, and she blew me off and suggested that I am out of my mind. She thinks that kids will ruin her career."

My mom paused. She starts singing. I know what that means.

"I told you that you should have discussed this before you got married. However, you can adopt a child."

"Maybe, Mom, but I have bigger issues. We are having marital problems."

"What kind of problem? You need to go see a counselor. You

cut me out of your life, so I don't intervene anymore."

"This cannot be solved by a counselor. I think she is having an affair. Casey stays out late at night and sometimes she does not come home at all."

"How is that possible, Daniel? I taught you better than this. You need to stand up for yourself. If you play a second figure in the home, she will treat you accordingly."

At that point, I realized that my mother was right. I gave Casey the latitude to do whatever she wants. I convince myself that her actions were beneficial to her job and any intervention might affect the flow. This was to my detriment.

"I am going to act, but I need time to figure things out. I want to visit North Carolina at the end of the month to clear my head."

"We are here for you whenever you want to come. Take your time to figure things out. I want to say I told you so, but now is not the time."

"OK, Mom, I will talk to you soon."

I always enjoy talking to my mother. It is refreshing to know that people still care for me. I spend so much time in this hostile environment that I convince myself that this is the norm. Sometimes I wonder why Casey got married. She only cares about her career and believes that anything else can wait. I was greedy. I place material things over my happiness. It was my actions that convinced Casey that I could be bought.

At work, there was a large function. We introduce a new model to the world. The president believes that I did a great job. He indicated that he wanted to have a word with me after the function. In my acknowledgment, I praise my production team for their hard work. After the function, we were having champagne when the president walked over to me.

"You are going places young man."

"Thank you, sir. We could not have done it without your support and the hard work of my team."

"I want to run something by you. One of my vice presidents will be retiring in a couple of months. We believe you would be a good fit for the position. You would be responsible for three states, but you would be based in New York."

"Thank you, sir, that would be great. Maybe I need a new environment and a fresh start."

"Take your time and discuss it with your family and let me know your decision by the end of the month.'

"I will."

It is as if my boss knew of my problem. The problem at home is showing in me. I am taking a week off. I will fly to North Carolina to share the news with my family and friends. I know Taylor will be happy for me. I do not know if my time in California is over. The next few months will determine my next move. I am not ready to give up on my marriage, but I am not willing to remain unhappy for the rest of my life. I will fight for the cause. When life says enough is enough, I will listen.

CHAPTER 29

Coming home to visit was a breath of fresh air. Everyone was happy to see me. Taylor and Brandon met me at the airport. We reminisce about the good old days. It was not about the days ahead, but the good times that we missed. It was like visiting heaven. Leaving my troubles behind and basking in a pure atmosphere where milk and honey flow.

Taylor looked great. She was in the area for a conference and took a few hours to see me. Her smile was like roses. Her smell reminds me of Christmas. Happy times. It was magical. Reminding me of my youth visiting Disney World with my parents. We were cheerful. There were no dull moments. Taylor's kisses bring sparkles to my eyes. She held me so gently. I see this gentle flower for who she is. A beautiful woman with a charming personality. Taylor has a caring soul that manufactures a world of compassion.

Brandon saw how she acts around me. He could not wait for her to leave to rub it in my face. The tension of our connection was evident from miles.

"Wow, dude," Brandon shouted. "This woman adores you. I watch the way she kisses you. The emotions that she shows for your plight, and the way she looked at you."

"Stop it, man, I am a married man now. She is just a nice person. I am not like you," I joked.

I pushed him to the side. Waiting for Taylor to disappear. I watched every step that she took. Her friendship meant so much to me. I was hoping that Brandon wouldn't notice. He had a microscope on me. He put me on trial.

"Go on, player. I see what you are doing. You are around me too long. Some of my characters are rubbing off on you."

"You wished. I am nothing like you."

I jumped on his back. It was joyful to see two adults playing in the airport parking lot. He was carrying me on his back like a donkey. It wasn't easy because I had gained a couple of pounds. He struggled, but it was fun.

Brandon dropped me off at my parent's house. This is where I will be staying for the week. I want twenty-four hours of rest and then I can take on the world. It felt like the world was on my shoulders. Carrying this burden wasn't easy. At some point, I need to let go. But now is not the time. My parents were happy to see me. Mom cooked beef and broccoli soup. I was ready to devour it. I know it was a symbol, but I didn't mind. Growing up, my mother only cooked soup when we were sick. My marital problems are sickness, and this type of medication can cure them. We sat around the table. We hold hands and pray. It reminds me of the olden days. Mom believes that a family that prays together, stays together.

"How is life treating you, boy?" Dad asked.

Was this a trick question? I didn't know how to answer. It was not clear if he was asking about my relationship or life in general.

"Life is kicking me from one corner of the earth to the next," I answered.

"I am glad that I grew you to be tough. Life can be hard sometimes. I can assure you that you will live."

"I hope so, pops. Life has not been treating me so kindly. I guess it is one of the features of being a man."

I was glad about the talk. My father is not the gentlest of giants, but that is the softest I am going to get out of him. Mom was observing. I know that her time will come. Her approach is different. She is more detailed and will pounce when the time is right.

"We are happy to see you, Dan," my mother uttered.

"Thank you, Mom. It is great to see my parents. I promise that I will not stay away so long ever again."

"You better not, or we will not let you back into this house. You hear me, boy?"

We all laughed. My mother got up from her chair and hugged me. Then kissed me on the top of the head.

"We love you and we are proud of what you have become. Whatever life throws at any of my children, we will be here to help you get through it."

I got emotional. Not sad, but happy to know that I have awesome parents to support me in times of need. My vulnerability allows my wife to encourage me to abandon my parents. This was a bridge that I should not have crossed. It is not too late for course correction. My eyes were watery. I was reminded of a mother's love. Never take it for granted.

"I have some news to share with you that might change my life forever."

My mother looked at me with skepticism and walked back to her seat.

"Not again, I do not think we can take any more bad news. Please save it for another time. Let us enjoy the time we have with you. Things will work themselves out."

"No, no, Mom, it is nothing like that. My boss offered to promote me to vice president. The position will be in New York. I have two months to decide. I want your views."

My father starts clapping and laughing and singing "Amazing Grace." It was like a church sermon. Mother burst into tears and started crying openly. Quickly, she was on the floor praying with both hands on my head.

"Deliverance!" she shouted. "God, I know you never failed us. I know you will come through for me. We ask you to protect him. You promised that you would, and you delivered."

I know my parents were Christians, but this was the first time that they were so spiritual.

"I guess you think I should take the position. Your actions speak louder than words."

It was like their answers were rehearsed. They sang it like active members of their church choir.

"Yes," my parents shouted.

"From the day you stopped coming home, your father told me that something was wrong. I was naive. I defended you all the time. I told your dad that you got caught up with your new job. I was convinced when you stop calling often. When we called, you told us that you cannot talk now. It was hard to admit to your father that he was right. We start praying. We prayed for you every night asking God to deliver you from your current problem."

"I was surprised at the offer too. I did not tell Casey. Even if I wanted to tell her, she didn't have time to listen."

"We do not care how you fixed your marriage if it can be fixed. But we want you to explore what life has to offer."

"I will communicate my decision to the company as soon as I get back to California."

My parents were happy. Dad started clearing the table. My mother was singing in jubilation. They were not interested in talking to me anymore. I read the room. I needed the rest anyway.

I went into my room. It brings back memories. Tears were flowing down my chin. It was raining from the inside. The thought of freedom felt good. My parents figured out that I was unhappy and brought my problems to the Lord in prayer. I feel relieved.

For the next few days, I slept like a baby. Relaxing at my parent's house like I was at a hotel. They told me that they would go easy on me this time. I take advantage of the situation. I have several places to visit before I go back to California. I want to visit my house. The tenant is in it, but I want to drive by. I didn't realize that my parents repainted the house. I could see it from a mile away. The grass was green and well-manicured. I drove passed slowly and waved at it as if it was a person. The house did not wave back. It, too, felt abandoned. My own house didn't remember me.

I went to see Taylor. She was happy to see me. Taylor ran from the building as soon as the receptionist announced that I was outside. She held me close. It was so tight I could not breathe. I was dying but I didn't want her to let go. For a married man to say that he was longing for a woman's touch was an exaggeration. She was touching me so gently like I was an egg.

"I will not break I assured you," I whispered to Taylor.

"I am not so sure. You are going through a lot. I want to treat you with care."

"Maybe I deserve that."

I told Taylor about the job opportunity in New York, and she was ecstatic. Jumping up and down like she just won the hundred-meter race at the Olympics. I could see the joy in her eyes. A perfect soul that was happy for me. She took my hands and rested them on her face.

"I am happy for you, Dan. You need a break. Maybe this will

improve your marriage. Happiness for me is to see good people make it."

"That is so sweet of you to say. God knows why he places you in my path. You are a true friend. The sweetest woman I know."

We were caught up in the moment. I wanted to kiss her so badly. I could see that she wants the same thing. But she is so disciplined. I closed my eyes and was moving closer for the kiss. With my arms around her waist, I pulled her closer. In the heat of the moment, I felt her index finger pressed against my lips.

"You are a married man, Dan Walker. I will not help you to destroy your marriage."

Taylor shuffles out of my arms. This was the first time that I didn't remember my ring. Taylor was made from a special cloth. She is a woman with class and character. We sat in her room and talked for hours. I couldn't sleep over because my mother is strict.

It is my time to leave North Carolina. I should leave in the shadow of darkness. I am going home to my wife. However, that thought brought sadness. I was hoping for the journey to be longer. I am leaving everything that makes me happy. Life in my home state will never be the same. California is a great state. I wonder why it has been so unkind to me. The world demands perfection and I intend to give it my all. I have a job to do. It is going to be hard, but I will try. I will save my marriage. I do not promise a miracle, but I will take control of my life. I hope for a change that Casey will be home waiting for me. It is just a thought.

CHAPTER 30

Back in California, everything remains the same. I came home to an empty house. Something was unusual. The house had this strange smell. It was the smell of tobacco. It was evident in the kitchen, bedroom, and patio. The remnant of cigarette butts could be seen in the backyard, driveway, garbage, and the bin in the bathroom. It was welcoming. Not the welcome that I was hoping for. None of us smoke. I did not say anything. How much more can I take? The river is overflowing. At some point, the dam will break. The flood is evident.

I went through the week with a heavy heart. I accept the offer at work. I need to start preparing for my next voyage. Several times, I tried to have a serious conversation with Casey, but every time she brushes me off. We hardly speak. We no longer share common interests. Casey gets upset easily. I want to tell her about the job opportunity in New York. She deserves to know.

The house was noisy that Saturday. Casey was home. She came home a few hours ago. It was a departure from other days when she didn't come home. She was in the kitchen cooking breakfast. I was shocked that she remembered where the kitchen was. The eggs and sausages were talking from the bedroom. I was eager to sit and have breakfast with my wife. Casey sat and ate her food by herself. Finally, the call came.

"Dan, there is some breakfast in the pot. You can share some if you are hungry."

I was disappointed but humbled. I gave her latitude. I did not expect much from her. I am grateful that she cooked for me.

"Can you share it for me? My arms feel a little sore."

Casey hissed her teeth. It was so loud it could be heard from outside.

"You should be grateful that I cook for you. Any woman in my position would not be so generous."

"You are not any woman. You are my wife."

By this time, Casey was heading to the living room. She made a sudden turn and rushed back to the kitchen to empty the pot with the food in the garbage pan.

"There is no need to argue. Make your breakfast. You are an ungrateful man. I should be worshipped by you, not be treated like your helper."

The house went dark. The world went dark. Reality was staring me in the face. I do not need another episode to convince me that my marriage is over. We are just going through the motion.

"Why did you do that? You do not need to be so unkind. If there is something you want to say to me, I am here. It appears that we grew apart. Why did we get here?"

Casey took her purse and her car key and headed for the door. "I have no time to explain anything to you, and I do not have to."

She slammed the door, jumped in her car, and drove away. It was worse than I thought. How crazy I was to think that our marriage can be repaired. Casey lost all respect for me. This is now a marriage of convenience. I need to cut my losses and move on. Happiness was never guaranteed. The urge for a relationship is normal. Life is trial and error. I believe in destiny, but we do not know about our destiny. Life is what I make it to be. If I stay here, Casey will treat me like nothing. I place a value on life. I place value on myself. Love must start with me. I must love myself first before I can love someone else.

The next month was spent making provisions to move to New York. We hardly say anything to each other. Whenever she was there, we greeted each other like coworkers. Casey came home once per week. She indicated that she was working on a new project that would keep her away for the next two weeks. I nod my head in agreement because I know that I have a plan.

It was getting closer to crunch time. I shipped my two cars and my belongings to my new address in New York. Even if Casey was here, she wouldn't even have noticed that all my stuff was gone. After work, I went to see a lawyer. I decided to file for divorce. This was the hardest decision I have ever made. Even though it was obvious that Casey was dating someone else, deep down inside of me I thought that we could work things out. It was not possible. Casey would not give me the time of day. My presence became poisonous in the house. Every time I talk to her, my voice makes her irritable. The lawyer gave me several options including meeting with a marriage counselor with Casey. After explaining everything to her and the marriage counselor, they decided that it might be best for us to go our separate ways.

"Mr. Walker, your situation is dire. If you are telling the truth, this is the strangest behavior I have ever heard displayed by anyone. I have heard of people spending a night or two, but one week, two weeks is a stretch."

"We used to be in love. She was so kind to me. I was obedient to her, and she betrayed me."

This was a classic test case for both the lawyer and the family counselor. They listened to me in disbelief. They wondered how I stayed in the situation so long. It was easy. We committed to staying with each other until death. But there comes a point when

I realize that we reach the point of no return.

"What do you want out of this divorce? I can help you to reach an amicable settlement. Give me a list of assets that you both owned. I will work on the list and give you my recommendations within two days."

"Please stop. Stop right there. I am not ungrateful. Casey was kind to me. She bought me a lot of gifts. I am not interested in anything from her. I just want to file for divorce and move on. I want my life back. I have wasted three years of my life that I cannot regain. Now, I have an opportunity to dictate the future with someone else."

"You are a strange man with a good heart. This will be an easy case. I will file the divorce papers tomorrow, talk to the judge myself and have the bailiff serve your wife the divorce papers the next day."

"That sounds good madam, but I want you to work with my timetable. My final day at work is next week Wednesday. I will leave for New York the following day. I want you to serve the divorce paper the following Friday."

The lawyer and the family counselor looked at each other and laughed. They realized that I was not as foolish as Casey takes me to be.

"You want to be nonconfrontational and that is good," the lawyer points out.

"Yes, Madam," I replied.

"Consider it done."

We shake hands and pay my debt and pathways. It was supposed to be a sad occasion, but my heart was contented. I was smiling inside. I was relieved. I entered this marriage on my cognition, and I leave on the same term. Nothing will break my spirit for the next week.

On my way home, a drum was beating in my head. It was not loud enough to disturb me. It was singing freedom. Free at last. I am not taking a victory lap. Everybody deserves to be happy. They deserve to live in an environment where peace and sanity are promoted. I was like a road angel, being courteous to every road user. Blowing my horn excessively to people for no reason.

I inform all the important people in my life. Everyone believes that I did the right thing or openly supports my action. My parents are planning to visit me in New York in another month, once I get settled. Brandon gives himself an open invitation and even assigned one of my guest rooms to himself. My brother, Berkley, lives in New York and promised to help me unpack over the weekend.

Taylor was not jumping up and down, but I could tell from her voice that she was pleased.

"Who will help you to arrange the place? Men are not good at decorations. They tend to mismatch things. Most places need a woman's touch." Taylor explained.

"I think I will manage. My mother might be there next month to correct any error."

"Nonsense. I will not allow your life to be in disarray again. You need to start fresh. You need the right start. Tell you what. I will take one week off from my job and come to help you. I will not take no for an answer."

It was like listening to the voice of God. This must be a representative of God.

"I would love that very much."

The celebration is on. I live for this moment. It was as if I was wearing a visor at home. Nothing bothers me. My mind was clear. That night, I slept like a baby. Rehashing in my dream was the hope of meeting the lady in red. Understanding my decisions and being contented with the outcome.

Thursday was finally here. I have not seen Casey in one week. It didn't matter. I wanted to say goodbye to Pepper but he was at Casey's parents' house. California was once my home. It was bad in the beginning, and it remained the same in the end. I got the keys to the house from under the tire of the truck in the driveway, three years after, I left it in the same place when I was leaving. There were not many memories to wait around for, so I left the house and did not look back. It was like leaving prison after a long sentence. Joy came when the plane left the airport. Deliverance.

In New York, Taylor was at the airport waiting for me. She was wearing a red dress. I was breathless. It was the prettiest I have ever seen her. I recognize that dress. It was the dress in my dream. I was dreaming about Taylor all along. Our greetings were not normal. She sprung on me like a tiger waiting to devour her prey. We kissed. The kiss was passionate. It was emotional. She was crying on my shoulders.

"I spent four years chasing you away and almost lost you. This time, it will not happen again. If you allow me, I will stick by you for the rest of your life. We will raise a family together."

In a crowded airport, Taylor was proposing to me. I shouted "Yes" from the bottom of my lungs. I learn the hard way. Most people make the same mistake as I did. Mistaken love for infatuation. Falling for material things and ignoring the right person that was right before me from the start. I learn the hard way. Today I close a dark chapter in my life. Tomorrow, I expect Casey to sign the divorce papers. That will begin a new chapter in my life. A journey that should have been from the start. A life with Taylor. Tomorrow will see a new job, state, house, and a lifetime that I will embrace. I will embrace it with all my heart. I hoped to start a family. I will realize my dream.

CHAPTER 31

The first night in New York was ideal. Taylor and I spent all night rearranging the house to make it ideal. I observe her energy and I see her passion. Her effort tells it all. Taylor was doing it from her heart. The walls were empty. They were missing something. They were missing pictures of us. We want moments that we can cherish. We were exhausted and tired. Taylor fell asleep in my arms.

Friday will be a momentous day. We were not going to work so we could sleep the entire day if we wanted. The bailiff is expected to serve the divorce papers to Casey, and I want to be up for the notification. Taylor knew about the plan and hoped that Casey would sign the papers and move on. At the stroke of ten a.m., the bailiff walked into Casey's office and demanded to see her. After some hesitation, he forced his way into her office and served her with the papers. At five past ten in the morning, I was notified that the epistle was done. I thank them for their service. I knew it had just started.

I was notified shortly after that my wife broke into my old office looking for me. My boss informed her that I was not at work today. She jumped into her car and raced to the house. Casey was shocked that I wasn't there. She called me more than fifty times wondering where I was. Casey left some nasty messages for me. I wanted to let it set in. I want her to realize that her actions hurt me. After an hour, I answered the phone.

"Where are you? I need to talk to you right now. What kind

of sick game are you playing? You have the nerve to serve me divorce papers. Who the hell do you think you are?" Casey shouted.

Casey was screaming from the top of the mountain. She was in tears. She did not anticipate what happened.

"We are over Casey. Your actions have consequences. You moved on three years ago. We were just going through the motions."

"How dare you. It is over when I say it is over. What do you think my friends will say about me? You are trying to embarrass me."

Casey was losing her voice. Her behavior was obvious. She was losing her mind. Having a relationship where she believes that she is the queen, and I am the servant. It explains her actions. I need a partner, not a financier. Someone willing to work with me to achieve a collective goal.

"You take me for granted. There was no respect in the relationship all along. I was lonelier with you than when I was single."

"I demand that you come home right now. You are a coward. Face me like a man and tell me all these things to my face. I give you a week to crawl back into this house. You cannot survive in California without me."

"I am gone, it's over. I am not coming back. It was the worst three years of my life. You have a kind heart, but a terrible character. You need to learn to treat people as human beings. Until you learn to do that, you will chase every man away."

Casey was moving from room to room looking for my belongings. She screams louder when she discovers that nothing was there. The screams were getting louder. I turned down the phone and put it on speaker so that Taylor could hear what was happening. Even then, it was too loud for us.

"You bastard. You move out all your stuff without telling me. I am signing this paper now and taking it to your lawyer's office. I give you until tomorrow to come crawling back. Any time after that, it will be too late."

Casey hangs up and storms out of the house. Her behavior convinced me that I made the right decision. It was a bright day. A day that I want to cherish. I am waiting for the lawyer to call me. Once she signs the paper, I will have reason to celebrate. Taylor assured me that I have her support. She emphasizes that it doesn't matter how long Casey takes to sign the divorce paper, she will be there for me. I am grateful to her. My phone is ringing. The lawyer is calling.

"Hell madam, Dan here."

"Hi, Mr. Walker."

The lawyer was laughing. She was laughing so hard; I couldn't hear a word that she was saying. I started laughing too.

"I can see why you decided to divorce your wife. She pushed down my door. I was going to call the police. She tosses the divorce papers at my head. I hid behind the desk. She keeps screaming. 'See what you did. Are you proud of yourself? You are a woman and should know better. You single-handedly destroy a happy home. I will get you for this.' Casey threatened me in the presence of all my staff and assured me that she will have me disbarred from California."

"I am sorry to put you through this. Live is short and I deserve happiness."

"It is OK. She signed the papers and that is all that matters. I anticipate that she might try to stalk you for a couple of days. Do not share where you work or live with her. She appears to be a narcissistic woman. So, after a week, her pride will force her to move on. So, hang in there, and thanks for choosing us for your marriage business."

How did we get here? I was happy to call Casey's name every day. But it was not meant to be. Life is a journey. It takes me to California. Bounce me around a couple of times. I am stronger. I am wiser. My experiences taught me to be a better person. I just want to hold Taylor closer to me. I want to thank her for helping me through the most difficult time.

I just closed the last chapter of that book. It was a painful experience. This experience does not affect my ability to love. It prepares me to love more. I am opening a new chapter of a new book. This book will have unlimited chapters. I will have no reason to close it. Determination and self-preservation will be my friends. It encourages me to work hard on my relationship, but also tells me when it is over.

Taylor sat beside me through the entire episode. Curl up in my arms when it gets intense. She was quiet. She was uneasy. We need to celebrate. I kissed her. I stared into her eyes and told her how much I love her.

"We need to go out and celebrate. It is the beginning of a new life. I am single again. I am ready to get married again. Let us find the best restaurant in New York and celebrate." I try to convince Taylor.

"No, Dan, let us stay here and enjoy each other's company. I need to get to know you and you need to get to know me. Let us find comfort in each other's arms."

At that moment, I could not tell what time of day it was. I want this magic to last. Our bodies pressed against each other, making it impossible for anything to intervene. I feel like God is rewarding me for my effort. I feel so alive. This feels different. I know this is love. I closed my eyes, but I would see Taylor in the dark. Beauty tends to shine from the darkest room. Creating its light to allow me to find myself around.

I am not hungry. I am not in the mood to talk. If God gives me a choice to enter heaven right now, I might pass. The feelings of belonging were evident. Taylor wanted to spend some quality time together and she deserved that moment. I cannot remember if we ate all day. Love was in the air, and we wasted no time.

The next day, Casey called as usual. This time she was calm. It appears that reality is starting to set in. What a difference a day makes. Last week Casey refused to come home. Now she is home every day looking for me.

"I see you are still not here, Dan. I am done playing with you. You need to stop the games that you are playing and come home. If it is a new car you want, you can have it. Anything you desire, please let me know."

"Casey, I am not going to be ungrateful. But life is more than a gift. Even though I love the gift, I did not marry you for gifts. I marry you because I fell in love with you, and I was unhappy. I thought that you would make my life complete. But I was wrong. You grew me out. You did not see me as your equal."

"But I can change. I can be a better person. I can be the person you want me to be. Just come home and let us work this out."

"We did not make love for almost two years. We hardly see each other. You were dating other men and didn't care what I thought. You took a man into our matrimonial home. And all that, I thought that we could work it out. It took breakfast for me to realize that we are two different people and belong to a separate world."

"I do not know what got into me. I was more interested in my job and what goes on in the world. I tried to change you, but

I did not make any time for you. Can we put the past behind us? I admit that I messed up, but you didn't complain."

"I could not complain because you were not there for me to talk to. Even when you were there, you would not listen. You are a kindhearted person, and I know that one day you will make someone happy."

"I signed the divorce papers because I was upset. There was nothing that I was doing that caused me to think. If I thought that you were serious, it would not be signed. Let me know if you want me to come to North Carolina. I am willing to try."

"You are not listening to me, Casey. It is over. We do not love each other anymore. I realized that I made a mistake from the start. I married you for the wrong reason. Life is too short to stay around someone for the sake of it. I moved on with my life. Making the option that I should have made three years ago. I wish you all the best with your life."

I could hear Casey talking on the phone as I ended the call. There is nothing more to talk about. Win or lose, the war is ended. I will make peace from this day forward. A new day had dawned. I will not look back. My commitment to Taylor is to move forward, and I am loving it. We intend to put some plans in motion, but we are in no hurry. Life is like a drawing book, and we intend to draw the next chapter of our lives. We will do it together.

CHAPTER 32

The first week in New York was like a dry run. I settled in at the job and tried to get acquainted with the employees. My office is on the fifth floor overlooking the town center. The people are warm and friendly. They gave me several recommendations for the hot spots in town. I noticed a large building about ten blocks away. It was one of the chains of stores where Taylor worked. An idea came into my head. What if Taylor applies for a transfer from North Carolina to New York? That would be ideal. It would make us inseparable. I was eager to go home to explore my idea.

At home, Taylor prepares dinner for me. She loves New York but must go back to North Carolina for her job.

"Hey, honey, this crazy idea came across my mind today while some coworkers were giving me a tour of the city. I came across one of your stores which is located ten blocks from my office. What if you ask your boss for a transfer? Would that be possible?"

"I don't know if they would allow it, but it is worth a try. I have been working with the company for over ten years. They might be hesitant to let me go."

I like what I hear. If Taylor was on the same page, anything was possible.

"Can you call her now and explain that your fiancé just moved to New York, and you want to join him? Let us hear what she says."

I just turned on the bulbs in Taylor's eyes and they lit up like the stadium. She sprung from her seat without hesitation and retrieved the phone from her bag. The number was on the speed dial because the phone was ringing within seconds.

"Hi, Taylor, what time are you coming in on Monday?" her manager asked.

"It should be nine a.m., but that is what I am calling you about. I have a small request from you. I have worked with you for a long time, and you always encourage me to inform you if I see any job opportunities anywhere in the organization."

"Sure, I am all about employee development. Did you identify one?"

"No, not really but I was wondering if I can get a transfer to the New York office."

"Taylor, what is going on? You know we need you here. Furthermore, New York is the headquarters for the organization, and they do not offer retail operations."

At that point, my mood changed. It was hopeless. Taylor only has retail experience and may not be a good fit here. I start to brainstorm other options in my head.

"My fiancé just moved to New York. He is the guy I always talk to you about. He is my world and I love him. I want to spend the rest of my life with him and that includes joining him here. This is a great organization and I enjoy working here. I hope you can help me look to see if anything is possible."

"Dan? The same person that lives in California? I am confused."

"Yes, the same Dan Walker. It is a long story, and I will tell you all about it when I get there, but he was offered a senior position here. I do not want to mess it up this time."

"Oh, OK Taylor. Tell you what. My old boss works there in New York. Let me touch base with him and call you back. Say hi to Dan for me."

"Thank you. I will do that."

As she hangs up, Taylor gets down on her knees. We learn that for anything we want in life, we need to talk to God in prayer. It was positive and we hope that we can hear better news from the manager. Taylor clings to the phone for several minutes. She wouldn't move for anything. I reminded her that it was a mobile phone, and she could take it with her. After an hour's wait, we start to brainstorm other options. We started going through job sites to see if there was any vacancy that she might want. I also suggest that she can move here until she finds a job. My salary can take care of both of us. One way or another, we will be together.

I was in the TV room watching sports when Taylor came rushing in to inform me that her manager was calling back.

"Hello, madam, thank you for calling back."

"I spoke with the manager, and he confirmed my suspicion that there is no retail office in New York, and it would be difficult to facilitate a transfer."

I could see the disappointment on Taylor's face. She was looking confused. Trying to get her words out, but it wasn't happening. I was massaging her shoulders. Assuring her that everything will be fine. We will figure this out together.

"Thank you for your help and I will see you on Monday," Casey responded with disappointment.

"Wait, wait, wait, I am not finished," the manager interjected. "Tom said that his retail and inventory manager went on retirement on Friday, but there were several people prepared for the position. I advised him of your current situation, and he said to ask you to come in and talk to him on Monday."

Taylor's smile became bigger than the moon. She was

jumping up and down. The job was not given to her, but we are applauding the opportunity.

"I will be there, and I appreciate your kindness."

"I know that you know everything there is to know about retail but read up on inventory. I wish you all the best. Either way, I will see you next week."

Before she could hang up, Taylor was on the computer looking up everything about inventory.

"Dan, I do not want you to talk to me for the next six hours unless you are asking me something about inventory."

"We will do it together."

We were like astronauts searching everywhere on the web, printing and compiling the information. We went over them several times together until she understood the concepts. At midnight, Taylor declares that she was ready. This was extraordinary. She grasped all the concepts on inventory and was ready for any college exams. We went to bed because she wanted to get enough rest.

In the morning, Taylor was looking exquisite. I am looking for a new manager. She was intelligent and sharp. We rehearse on our way to work. Taylor stepped from the car with confidence. Capturing her audience with beauty and class. I could feel in my bones that she would get the job. The anxiety lingers for a few hours. I could not get anything done. I was waiting patiently for her to call. I was fixated on the window. I could see about seven blocks away.

About midday, I see some movement. My queen was approaching from half a mile away. She was sliding. It was a lesson. Taylor was teaching the people of New York how to walk. Beyoncé has nothing on her. The way she was strolling with an upward posture, I know she got the job. However, I couldn't wait for her to reach me. I jumped in the elevator and dashed downstairs. On the street, I could see that pretty smile from a mile away. I walked up to her.

"We did it, Dan, we did it. I execute myself like I was an inventory expert. Expounding on all aspects of the subject and using a parallel track to couple it with my knowledge of retail. Tom was so impressed with me that he called another senior manager to join him. I was in a talking mood. I did it all because of love. Every time I remember how much I want to be with you, it compels me to explain more. You are my source of strength.

"I am proud of you. God rewards us with whatever we asked of him. The more I looked at you the more I wanted you. It takes courage to do what you just did. You are a genius in your own right."

I could not find enough adjectives to describe Taylor. It is easy to explain love to anyone who wants to listen. If I explain how I am feeling toward Taylor, the author will be able to draw my feelings in words and deeds. It is comical to want someone so much. I am prepared to be a clown for her.

Since I left California, there has never been a dull day. Every day with Taylor feels better than the day before. Her energy is enough to light up an entire stadium. When we walked together, we walked with pride and moved with conviction. Today proves to us that we can achieve great things if we move together. It is the level of understanding that we have and the love that we share. We are proud of every moment together.

Irrespective of what Taylor says, this moment deserves a celebration. I took her to the restaurant next door. The waiter referred to us as Mr. and Mrs. Walker and we did not object. This time Taylor liked the title. She knows that soon, and very soon, the title will be bestowed upon her. We sat and the meal was served. The restaurant could have issued only one set of plates as Taylor was feeding me from her plate. It was beautiful. It looked beautiful. People were admiring us. Mimicking our every move.

I whisper a prayer in my mind asking God to let this last forever. It was painful to see Taylor go. She was going back to North Carolina to work out for the rest of the week. To put her house in order and ship her things home. I could not wait for her to come home. I missed her already. We were meant to be. The chemistry feels everlasting.

Taylor called me twice per day to check up on me. We talked on the phone every night until I fell asleep. She was the first voice I wanted to hear when I woke up, and the last voice when I went to sleep. The thought is beautiful. I cannot get it out of my head. Knowing that the next time I lay eyes on Taylor, she will be here with me forever. The birds in Central Park will get to know us together. I realized one thing. It is strange. Since Taylor came back into my life, I stopped dreaming. I crave the woman in red. My dream was realized. There is no need to dream again. To me, dreams no longer have meaning. I have it all. I ask for happiness and happiness to come. This is what it meant to fall in love. To miss the person every minute of the day. When she is not around the day seems long. When she is around, the hours are not enough. I believe that my love is a unity of purpose. It puts my body on edge. Like a ticking time bomb waiting to explode. Having a piece of mind when that special someone is around. I feel powerful. I want to give Taylor the world, even though it isn't mine. God will excuse me. He will understand that we were meant for each other. Taylor is coming home on Saturday. I feel like going to the airport two days in advance. I can't wait.

CHAPTER 33

Finally, Saturday is here. I am eager to go to the airport to pick up Taylor. The rain is falling. To me, this is an indication that the elements are cheering for me. Crying tears of joy. I do not need an umbrella. I am protected by love. Covered by the warm embrace from my relationship with Taylor. I check the clock in the kitchen every five minutes. It appears that the day is paused. Time is creeping up and I want it to go faster.

I arrive at the airport two hours before Taylor's flight is due, hoping that she would arrive earlier. I watched several flights arrive and depart. Couples wish their loved ones goodbye, while others welcome their families and friends. I try to find a vantage point where I can see everything that was happening. I was afraid to buy a drink or visit the restroom fearing that I might miss something. This is not the first time that I have picked up Taylor from the airport. However, this time was different because we will be living together for the rest of our lives.

At twelve fifteen, the iron bird landed. The plane taxis to its terminal gate. The Queen of New York departs. She was walking fast. Looking to her left, then to her right. Taylor was searching for something. I positioned myself at the bottom of the stairs to baggage claim, with my eyes fixated on the top of the stairs. Taylor was running down the steps. Once she saw me, she dropped the handbag and carry-on and dove into my arms. If the water was deep, she would manage the journey. If it was shallow, there was enough room to maneuver the jump. It did not matter.

I was prepared as a lifeguard to save her. It was joyous to see her again. We kissed. This was the day that I have been praying for.

The journey home was refreshing. Taylor wound down the window. The wind was blowing in her face, pushing her hair backward to display her beauty. Taylor positioned the seat backward and leaned on the side of the window. With her right hand protecting her face and her left hand clutching mine.

"Did you miss me, babes? I couldn't wait for the week to end so I could reach here. I start packing the moment I reach Greensboro," Taylor asserts.

"I have been counting down from the day you leave. How are your parents? Did you get to see them? I asked.

"They are doing fine. My father suggested that it was the happiest that he had seen me since my childhood. They are planning to visit us as soon as we settle."

Taylor looked so relaxed. It appears that she had no cares in the world. The weight is off her shoulders. She drops her guard. I have gained her trust and I will work to keep it. Life has taught me to be kind to people and they will be kind to me.

"I took some pictures that were at my house from the first day we met in person. I look a bit cuter then, but it might help us to remember where our journey starts."

"Let me see them, Dan. I can't believe that you still have them. You were supposed to throw them away when you got married."

"I couldn't muster the strength to throw them away. Luckily, I did not. They were my source of strength whenever I was down. It makes me smile every time I look at them."

I handed the pictures to Taylor. Immediately, she started laughing. She couldn't control herself. It shows the evolution of my body. The toll that four years of my last relationship had on me.

"We cannot put these at the front of the house, but they have a place on the wall. I might just cut you off. You look different. Visitors to the house might ask about this guy," Taylor joked.

It is amazing to see that Taylor looked the same. Glowing in the same pool of light as the day we met. As we parked in the driveway, the rain stopped. Two birds were on the grass hunting their meal. Playing with each other as if they just started dating. Our presence did not bother them. They were feeding each other worms. They were admirable. The birds remind us of ourselves. We opened the trunk of the SUV and sat on the tailgate. Taylor was sitting on my foot. We were watching the birds expressing their love for each other. With my arms around her waist, we are observing the sun fight to keep the rain away. The outside was beautiful. We were in no hurry to go inside.

Our neighbor saw us outside enjoying the atmosphere. They came over to introduce themselves. The man had a six-pack of beer in his hands and the woman with a beautiful anthurium flower.

"Hi, my name is David Skyers, and my wife Cathy. We live next door. We just want to welcome you to the community."

"Pleased to meet you. This is Dan, and I am Taylor. We love the neighborhood. It is nice and quiet."

Cathy handed the flower to Taylor who hugged it with one arm. Her head started looking in all directions trying to find the best place for the plant.

"It is an indoor plant. She might not do well outside," Cathy explained.

"Great, I have the perfect place for it. I will put it on my piano."

As we talk and try to get acquainted, David offers us some

beer.

"I am not a beer person, but I have a great bottle of wine inside that would be great for this weather," Taylor suggested.

"I am in," Cathy replied. "I am not a beer lover myself."

I took one of the beers while Taylor went inside to get the bottle of Merlot. It was a great start in a new community. These are hard-working people who enjoy each other's company. Taylor came back with two glasses and handed one to Cathy.

"As the saying goes, men love their beers," I joked.

There was loud laughter. An evening that was meant to be for us and the birds were spent getting to know the Skyers family. The rain decided that it had seen enough. There was a sudden downpour. Everybody scampers for cover. Our neighbor raced across the road while I provided cover for Taylor with my hands.

Taylor had her clothes to unpack, but she was in no hurry. The rain was beating on the window. Knocking on the door wanting to come in. Lightning and thunder started to light up the evening skies. I closed the blinds. The rain was humming outside. At times, it was singing louder. Taylor cuddles up in my arms, looking for protection. She is in the right place. She is safe. I am forced to compare relationships. Only to make it stronger. Taylor and I are different. We are a unit. We joined to form a common bond. This provides a level of comfort that was missing from my life.

The next day, Taylor woke up early. She was in the mood for decoration. We chose some memorable pictures. I went out to buy some frames while Taylor unpacked all her stuff. This is what unity looks like. It was easy to tell when you entered the house. We cherish all our memories. Imagine when the biggest memories are created. We might not have enough space to display them.

While at the store buying picture frames, I saw a blue shirt and a pair of shorts that matched it. It was so tiny. I was not looking for clothes, but my eyes were fixated on them. It was so cute. I wanted to buy it, but I decided against it. It was bothering me. There was this little female voice in my head bothering me about babies. I try to ignore the voice, but it keeps chanting to me. Finally, I decided to buy the suit. I never discussed family with Taylor, but I know that she wanted children. Maybe it is time for this conversation. I hid the baby suit behind the seat in my truck. I did not want Taylor to see it.

At home, Taylor was in a good mood. She was rearranging the house. In the background, she was blasting the stereo. Jumping from one corner of the house to the next. Dancing to the song from "Maniac of Love" by Michael Sembello. Sliding across the hall like the lady in the movie. She was a star. Star in her rights. It was an unproduced movie, but Taylor was willing to make it a success. Maybe a Netflix series. Whatever it was, she was in a great mood, and nothing would change that. Should I join in and steal her thunder? No. I am her backup singer, and I will stick to that role. I started humming songs and clapping. Cheering my princess as she performs the act of her life. Taylor loved it. She input more energy and brought the curtain down.

I wanted to do something special while Taylor continued working on the house. It might be a good idea to cook for her. Let us celebrate indoors and continue the red wine that she opened yesterday. I was preparing her favorite, sesame chicken with white rice and broccoli. I must be at my best. The first impression lasts for a lifetime. I know I was doing it right. The smell was taking over the house. I need to align the smell with the taste. If I do that, it will blow Taylor away.

After about two hours, the table was set. Two candles were

burning. One for the present and the other for the future. The wine was chill and ready for consumption. I emphasized this in the presentation. The rice occupies a third of the plate, the broccoli on a third, and the chicken on the other third. Time leaves and dried season was used to decorate the plate.

I invite Taylor to join me in the dining room. She was impressed. I was playing "Just Once" by James Ingram in the background.

"Wow! Wow! I am impressed. I love when my man cooked for me. You went all out. You cooked my favorite meal. You earn my heart with the presentation. Let me taste it."

I was nervous. My heart was pounding in my chest. I want the food to taste good. If it is even for this one time. She took the first bite and swallowed it. She eats another piece. She paused. Maybe she didn't like it. Then the fork was getting busy.

"Honey, do you like it?" I asked the question, but I didn't want the answer.

"No, I don't like it, I love it. Let me have some more. Make sure you have enough if I want to eat a third time."

"I have enough for you, babes."

I pour Taylor some wine and some for myself. She was grateful for my effort. We sing and dance all night. There were not long enough songs that we did not dance to. It was an eventful evening. We deserve more evenings like this. The world is ready for us, and we are ready to face the world. Our parents will be coming here next month to visit. We are settled. We are prepared for them.

CHAPTER 34

It has been two months since we moved to New York. Life is great. Taylor brings lunch for me every day. She didn't mind making the ten-block journey to see me. It is an opportunity for us to spend time with each other. Sometimes we catch a movie during lunch or visit the parks or museums. There is never a dull day for us.

This weekend we will be hosting our parents. It is overdue and they are eager to come and see us. This was the first time that both our parents would get to know each other. It will be Thanksgiving and so we are planning a large festivity. We also invited my brother and the next-door neighbors. Before the festivity starts, my parents arrive. They were happy to see us. My mom wanted to help, but we convinced her that we have things covered. Everything was set for inside because it was getting cold in New York. My mother was lingering around the kitchen. She always has a passion for Taylor.

"Has he been treating you good, my child? Please let me know. He is not too old to get a beating from me."

"He is a good man, Mrs. Walker. I keep him under tight wrap."

"Call me Mom. You don't have to be so formal. We are a close-knit family and learn how to take care of each other."

"I could love that, Mom. Do you care to try my punch? It is to die for."

"Sure, what is in it? Young people are always tempted to

sneak something in the drink that is too strong for me."

"This might be good for you. It consists of lemon juice, red syrup, strawberry, crushed ice, and Jamaican rum."

Taylor poured some of her famous punch and handed it to my mother. She put a small amount in her mouth and tasted it. Then, my mother turns the entire glass to her head and finishes it with one swoop. It was obvious that she loved it.

"Take your time, Mom. The evening is long, and we need you around for dinner," I suggested.

My mother started tugging my shirt. Urging me to get her another glass of punch. I could not say no to my mother. My father and brother were on the other side of the hall treating themselves to some beers. The final guest to arrive was Taylor's parents. They were the newest addition to the family. Taylor and I met them at the door. They hugged and kissed us. They were happy to see the entire family together.

"Whose son dares to take away my only child from North Carolina to live in New York?" Taylor's dad shouted.

"If that is a good thing, then it is our son. But, if taking Taylor here is a bad thing, then, it is Mrs. Walker's child," my father joked in response.

"It is the best thing that has happened to my daughter. Pleased to meet you. Taylor told me so much about you."

Our parents were getting acquainted. Joking and laughing at each other's jokes. We left to get the turkey ready. There were about ten people and a lot of food. The table was set, and we were ready to eat. My mother prayed for the food. There was this weird request or suggestion in my mother's prayer that drew laughter from the room. She predicted that we will be meeting in a similar setting soon and asked God to hasten our steps.

"Hey, Mom, was that a suggestion or a request? Why are you

bothering God? He was a very busy man."

"When I look around this room, all I see is love. We have met together several times before, but this time is different. I can feel the comrade in the room."

As we started eating, it was a common sentiment around the room. I looked at Taylor and she stared at me. I could see the innocence in her eyes. Waiting for the right moment to say yes. Yes, to a life together to be my wife. We are not in any hurry. But let's be clear. It does not mean that we should string this issue along. I know that we will discuss it soon. My mother is smart. She starts the conversation with the hope that we will finish it. It is admirable to see our families come together in this fashion. Look at the smiles on everybody's faces. It tells a lot. This is the position where we find ourselves in. I move closer to Taylor and draw her closer. My action is to reassure her that I have her back. The way we looked at each other was evident.

My mother seems happier than normal. It seems like Taylor's punch is having an impact on her. I know that was not the case. My mother always loves Taylor. She believes that people should be free to choose the person they want to marry. If she had her wish, I would not have married Casey. But I learned from my mistake. It makes me stronger.

It was noticeable that Taylor was not doing the Thanksgiving dinner to earn the approval of anyone. She is a believer in family values and demands that we should build a strong family bond. What a difference from my previous marriage. Casey encouraged me to shut out my family from our lives. This was done to my detriment. I will never let that happen again.

Taylor whispered in my ear. She wanted me to thank everyone for coming. I did not want to do it. She pinched me in my side, and I jumped up. Once on my feet, I got the attention of the entire table. I have no other choice but to say something.

"I want to thank both sets of parents who are here today to join us for the weekend. We have wanted this moment from the day we moved here. We believe that our love and development should happen in stages. Each stage should include our parents who we expect to supervise our progress. We love each other and we love you too."

"This is a great house, but you can make it a great home. A home is full of life. Many lives. Big life and small life," my mom declared.

Everybody finds her statement funny. They were laughing. I know what she was saying. Taylor was pointing at me jokingly.

"Mom, please stop. Dad, get Mom to leave us alone!"

"Your mother needs those grandbabies. I cannot fault her for that."

Everybody starts to chant "more grandbabies, more grandbabies." Taylor uses her hands to cover her face. I am taking the pounding. No one helped me. The demonstration is getting louder. I love my family. They joked about the things that they wanted. Who could blame them for that? Taylor rises to my rescue. She picked up the jug with the punch and started around the room. People got distracted. Everybody wants to sample the punch. It was good. My mother could attest to it as she was on her third glass. Most people abandon their beers for punch.

It was a good idea to get to know each other. Our parents bonded very well. After dinner, they got together and helped us clean up the kitchen.

"Mom, we are OK. We can clean up the kitchen. You all get some rest," Taylor stated.

"Nonsense," my mother replies. "We are no longer strangers. We must help in whatever you do. We asked to visit because it is our first time here. But make no mistake, we will be here whenever we want to, going forward," my mother lamented.

"We are making an open invitation," Taylor's mom interjected.

It was clear that they were not going anywhere, so we joined and cleaned up the kitchen. It was a long day, so we retired to bed early. Our parents were staying in the two guest rooms downstairs and my brother was occupying the spare bedroom upstairs. They were not ready to retire to bed. We left them in the living room. We could hear the loud laugh echoing through the house. We were tired so we fell asleep.

The next day my brother took us to New York City to see two Broadway plays. He was more familiar with the area, as we were still learning. We were unaware of what we were doing, but we were clinging to each other every step of the way.

"Taylor is not going anywhere. I assure you that kidnappers do not work during the daytime so you can allow her to breathe." Berkley joked.

"I am taking no chances. It is better to be safe than sorrowful. I am so used to having her by my side that I am uncomfortable when she is not there," I responded.

Our parents were pleased with my responses. They believe that we belong together. My parents were convinced that God put us together. I know that God has a hand in our relationship. But whoever put us together, we are grateful. They may be married for more than twenty years, but they start to emanate our behavior. We are in love. We enjoy each other's company, and our chemistry is natural. As we move across the hall from one theater to the next, my basic instinct emerges. It is now a part of me to provide security for Taylor. I am her bodyguard, and she is my guardian angel.

The weekend was coming to an end. Everyone was departing in their own directions. My parents hugged and kissed us like we were toddlers. Kisses were flying all over the place. They were content.

My parents were confident that we would have everything under control. They were leaving happier than when they came.

"We will be back soon. I like New York. We might just buy a house here. Not next door, but within walking distance," Taylor's father suggested.

"Our home is your home. You are welcome to stay here if you want. No need to buy a house here," I suggested.

"I might just take you up on that offer."

They depart. The whole house is now empty. It is just me and Taylor again. One would believe that we would get lonely and sad. We missed our family, but we missed our time alone more. The vehicles were hardly out of sight and we couldn't wait to pounce on each other. I hold Taylor from behind and lift her in the air. My right hand was tickling her side. She was kicking like a mule. Laughing uncontrollably. Taylor wrestles out of my hands and escapes. She rushes into the bedroom and tries to close the door. I was faster than her. The monster captures his prey. I threw her on the bed and launched at her. We bumped foreheads. Not an accident to send us to the emergency room, but one that gathers laughter. We are very playful. We enjoy playing with each other.

CHAPTER 35

Time is moving fast. Taylor and I have lived together for almost a year. It was evident that my mother will look like a fortune teller. My mom tees the golf ball and expects me to hit it over three hundred yards. It requires practice, but I am ready. We have been talking for a while. Taylor is not interested in a large wedding, and I do not want to repeat the charade of the past. She prefers a small service with close family members. It looks like a repeat of our Thanksgiving dinner last year.

It will be a October to remember. The day is set for the wedding and the guest list is out. We opt for about fifty people. This is just a celebration because we have been acting as a married couple for a long time. It is not a traditional wedding. Our parents wanted a splash, but we ruled against them. They respected our wishes.

The night before the wedding, we refuse to follow customs. Taylor declares that she is not leaving my side. It was a big day and I wanted her to be the first person that I saw when I woke up in the morning. Our life will continue on the same trajectory. Only Taylor's last name will change. Her ring is beautiful. She loved it. Both rings slept on our pillows that night. We kept watching them. Nothing is going to happen to them.

"Dan, let us make this day more memorable. We will count down to midnight. At twelve one, we will declare the day officially our wedding day."

"I am in. We want this to be the best twenty-four hours of

our lives."

While our guests were downstairs entertaining themselves, we sat on the bed playing card games. Taylor won most of the games, but it didn't matter. Our objectives were to have fun. We were also playing music from my phone through a smart speaker. We get alternative selections. The fun is for us to know each other's songs. We were having fun. We sang out loud. My mother heard soul music from downstairs and rushed upstairs. There was a loud knock on the door.

"Open the door. It is the night before your wedding, for God's sake. There will be no hanky pranky going on in this house," my mother shouted.

We burst out laughing. The music was blasting, but it was sending the wrong signal.

"The door is open, Mom. We are here playing a game and listening to music," I suggested.

My mother opens the door. She wanted to open it wider, but the wall would not allow it. She has this innocent smirk on her face. She believes that she has just foiled a potential crime from happening.

"Keep the door open. You are not married yet. Reserve your energy for tomorrow. We have our eyes on you."

It was as if we weren't living together for a year. As we explained the game to my mom, she got interested. She asked Taylor's mom to join the game. Our fathers force their way into the room too and start participating. We end up with a generation divide. Most of the songs that we chose were not known by our parents. They close with some good songs. Old hits but they have meaning. My room became a karaoke spot. It was like a church choir. Everybody became professional singers. My father was singing like he was auditioning for a record deal. We were passing the mic like a group. I got a chance to serenade Taylor. Singing "One in a million" to her from one knee. I got a standing evasion.

As the night got later, we were watching the clock. We wanted to count down to a new day. Our parents realized that they overstayed their welcome in our room and left. The time was approaching. We had sixty seconds to make history. Our phones were recording. We were holding hands and counting down aloud. At the stroke of midnight, we kissed. It lasted for one minute. Our wedding date is here. We kneeled at the bedside, held hands, and pray to God for success. Taylor fell asleep on my chest.

At the church were our parents and the marriage officer. The ceremony was short but deliberate. The pastor emphasizes love and what we can do to make the magic last. It is official. Taylor is now my wife. She looked relaxed. Taylor was confident that we could build a relationship that could withstand any problem. Her finger was beaming. The diamond ring was calling her name from a distance. The moment is surreal. We were creating moments that will last forever.

Everyone was waiting for us at home. The limousine was full. We were in the middle with our parents to the left and right of us. It was symbolic. We wanted to show that we are all in this marriage together. Following the footsteps of our parents. Taylor's dress was exquisite. It was a small deviation from the traditional wedding dress. She was wearing my favorite color. The dress was built to fit. The fabric complements her figure and highlights the moment that we want to share. Her face was stunning. Taylor was made for this day.

The pandemonium begins. The photographer was capturing every move that Taylor made. She was gliding in thin air.

Allowing the wind to manipulate her hair as she walks with attitude. Taking gentle steps to avoid leaving me behind. I was proud to walk beside her. It was difficult for me to be her equal. Emotionally we are one, but her elegance stands out. I feel like I own the world.

The caterers set up tents in the backyard. They decorate the entire surroundings with red roses placed on the head table. The bands play light instrumentals. They create a magical moment where the background music touches our hearts. The food was tasty. This is a celebration like no other. The emotions in the room were high. Our parents were crying. These were tears of joy. Taylor's parents were happy to see their daughter get married. They knew that she was in good hands. They express gratitude to us for allowing them to be a part of the celebration.

"I watched my daughter grow up into a decent young lady. She starts dating at the age of nineteen. When it did not work out, she withdrew herself from the rest of the world. We thought she would never date again. The first time Dan came into her life, we realized a change. She was scared. She pushed him away. When he got married, she took it hard. Taylor blames herself for the decision that Dan took. We are happy about this day. We are proud of what she became, and I know she will be an awesome wife," Taylor's mom explained.

She was crying. The moment was joyous. Taylor gets up from her seat and hugs her mom. She was rubbing her back to comfort her. Taylor's mother holds her tight. Understanding that she will lose her daughter forever. It is my job to assure her that I will take care of her. I plan to do that. Taylor helped her to her seat, placing her mom in the hands of her father. It was my mother's turn. The words could hardly come out of her mouth. Knowing that she made a speech four years ago and it did not work out. My mother was cautious. Tears were flowing from her eyes. My dad was there to provide support.

"Today, I officially adopted a daughter. For us, she is special in this family. Our job is to make sure that they are happy. I know my son. I grew him. He is a good man, and he will make us proud. I remember when he was depressed and needed our support. We were always there for him. His friends provide moral support. He has grown into an awesome man. I watch the way Dan and Taylor look at each other. I observe how they treat each other. We are convinced that they were meant for each other. This is the happiest day of our life. Our little boy is finally happy."

My father was wiping her tears. Helping her to express her approval of us. We confide in each other. We love our parents and look to them for guidance. It was time for me to express myself. Taylor stands and holds my hand. Providing moral support while I talk. I am nervous. I understand the gravity of the situation. I am coming out of a failed marriage. I must convince the world that this one is different. Taylor whispered in my ear.

"You can do it, baby. Just be honest and express how you feel. They know that you are honest in your approach. There is no need to impress them," Taylor points out.

I was at ease. My heart starts beating normally again. She helps to boost my confidence. Standing by my side was all I needed.

"Today, I got married to the most beautiful woman in the world. In my mind, she is perfect. She has all the qualities that any man could want in a woman. I love her very much and was happy to marry her. I know that I have walked this path before. For that, I must convince her parents that this time is different. It is fine to be skeptical, but I learn from past experiences. I have great parents who have been married for over thirty years. They held strong through thick and thin. They are my role models. I should have used their expertise as a guide, but I shut them out of my life. I learn from my mistake. I will call on both our parents for guidance. There is no turning back. Taylor is my life, and I will keep my commitment to her."

At one point, my voice was breaking. I paused for a moment. I was staring into Taylor's eyes. Her smile was bright. She believes in me. Taylor held down my head and kissed me. That kiss pushed the words from my mouth.

"I want to thank our families for supporting us through this journey. They are a permanent part of our lives. To my friends, coworkers, and neighbors, thank you for your kind support. I am eager to dance with my wife, so I want to stop talking now."

There was a large cheer. Everybody was happy for us. The music started playing. I took my wife's hand and lead her to the center of the yard. I held her close to me. The music hypnotizes me. We were spinning and turning and enjoying the moment. Taylor was safe in my arms. She wasn't scared to lean over backward because she knew that I wouldn't let her fall. Mrs. Walker was championing the moment. I did not want to let her go. Taylor's father requests a dance, but I deny it. I was getting selfish. He understood. I cannot get enough of her.

The evening was electric, and the sun set on the activity. The outside was beautiful. We were watching the stars appear. They were reflecting the color of Taylor's dress. The atmosphere was chilly, but no match for our body temperature. We could feel the dew on our faces. Time flies when we are having fun. Our parents will be here for another week. We are leaving tomorrow for our honeymoon at Sandals Ocho Rios, Jamaica.

All good things must come to an end. Taylor was grateful for the day. She was walking around with some small bags of souvenirs and handing them to everyone and thanking them for their support. Our names will be everlasting. They will be in the company of our family and friends forever. We want to be a beacon of light for couples around the world. We should be on the lips of people who talk about love. The road is long, but we are prepared for the journey. We are confident that time will be kind to us.

CHAPTER 36

As we land in Jamaica, we were transported on a tour bus to the hotel. We sat in the third row close to the window. Our love was on tour. We are in a foreign country, but our relationship remains the same, sticking close to each other as we watched the shoreline to the hotel. Taylor was eager to bask in the sun. We rush to the room and leave our luggage. It was about two p.m. and the weather was perfect for swimming. Taylor transformed into her two-piece bathing suit, while I had on a pair of shorts. Taylor lies on the beach chair while I cover her entire body with sunscreen lotion. We stroll along the white sand beach with the seawater as blue as the sky. We hold hands and hunt for shells. I was like a tour guide. Mimicking the move that I did at the altar. I held the tip of her fingers and led her into the water. She was cold. I could see the cold bumps forming on her hands. She was trembling. Like an elephant, I gather some water with my hands and splash it on Taylor. She screamed. I splashed more. She tries to run away. It was difficult to run from me in the water. Taylor swam away like a fish. The lifeguard ensured that we stayed within the lines where the water was below our shoulders. We spent the rest of the evening swimming. We retire for the evening knowing that we have another six days to repeat the same process.

For the next six days, we explore all the amenities at the hotel including socializing with the local people. We were interested in the local dialect and the dance. Each night, we would join other guests in the hotel clubhouse where we would display what we know. We had a lot of fun and were sad when it had to end. We have a long life ahead of us and will certainly visit again next year. Our relationship deserves a yearly honeymoon, and we intend to take it.

It is more than three months since we got married. We develop some good habits to keep our relationship vibrant. One of my favorites is movie night. We visit the theater every Tuesday night to watch our favorite movies. Every time we are more childish than the week before. Hugging each other closer than the day before. Laughing at each other's jokes and feeding each other popcorn. This Tuesday, I observed that Taylor was eating more than normal. In my mind, she had missed lunch. I remembered that we had lunch together. Taylor fell asleep in the middle of the movie. I watch her sleep. When the movie finished, I woke her up.

"Taylor, time to go to your bed. Was I that boring today? You missed the entire movie. Worst, you ate all the food."

Taylor was laughing at herself. She still looks sleepy. Her eyes were half open. She balanced on my shoulders to the car.

"I don't know what happened to me today. I just feel tired. Maybe I eat too much. Next week I will let you eat first."

"Well, you eat for both of us." That was fine as I did not feel hungry.

We hardly reached home when I observed Taylor head to the bedroom. Before she changed into her pajamas, she fell asleep. I observed this behavior for a few weeks. Taylor told me that she almost falls asleep at work. When we met for lunch some of her habits were evident.

"I find myself eating between meals. You know that I watch how I eat. But something is wrong. I get hungry easily." Taylor points out.

"Maybe you are too comfortable. I need to create havoc in the house and increase your stress level." I joked.

I remembered something from a TV show I was watching some months ago. The man's wife's habits change. After weeks of investigation, they discovered that she was pregnant. I looked at Taylor and started smiling. I observed her from head to toe. There was nothing abnormal, but I was getting excited.

"What is so funny? Why are you looking at me like that? You are scaring me. I am not in the mood for your jokes."

"It is nothing. Just a thought."

"Dan, what are you thinking about? Share it with me. Are you keeping secrets from me? Please do not start now."

Taylor was curious about what I was thinking. I do not want to raise my hope and be wrong.

"In the movie we watched last week, the lady was displaying the same symptoms as you. It turns out that she was pregnant."

Taylor opens her eyes wider than the door to the restaurant. Wanted to smile, but she was not sure what to do. She pushed the plate to the side and turned the glass of water to her head. Taylor places her right hand on her stomach trying to feel if something is moving inside.

"I do not know, honey. Maybe I am just tired from working these long hours. However, I am taking nothing for granted. I have an appointment at the doctor's tomorrow to have a checkup. Maybe I should do a pregnancy test too."

"I will accompany you. Just let me know when you are ready, and I will come to pick you up."

"It is about five blocks from here. We can walk. I know we want children. But take this for what it is now until I do a test. I do not want you to be disappointed."

I did not know what to say. The thought of Taylor being

pregnant is worth celebrating. I am nervous. I will save my fire until I know more.

It was time to return to work. I walked Taylor to her office. This time I was more careful. I would not allow a fly to come close to her. At work, I could not concentrate. My mind was all over the place. I find myself thinking about baby clothes, strollers, daycare, and toys. I don't know if I should pray. I am confused.

At home, Taylor was pretending as if nothing happened. It was business as usual even though she was still displaying strange habits. She went to bed early. I couldn't sleep. I felt that if I closed my eyes, something would happen to her. I hugged her, but not too tight. I was cautious. This was the longest night. I did not want to watch a movie as I didn't want to wake Taylor. I sat there looking at the ceiling, talking to myself and hoping for a miracle.

I did not go to work as the effort would be futile. This time requires my undivided attention. Taylor was at work. I am getting ready to meet her. The traffic is heavy, but I have enough time. I parked outside her office and texted her to let her know I was there. Walking to the doctor's office was not an option. Taylor reminds me that she feels fine.

"Do not expect the unexpected. If I am pregnant, I would be happy. I do not feel pregnant."

Taylor was talking to me, but it was useless. I did not hear a word that she said. My ears were numb. My brain freezes. We walked into the doctor's office and sat down. The doctor was pleased to see me. He has no idea why I was there. After doing all his tests, I looked at Taylor and beckoned to the doctor.

"Is something wrong?" the doctor asked.

"Dan believes that I might be pregnant because my sleeping

and eating habits changed. He wants you to run a pregnancy test. It might be useless, but I want to see if my husband is right."

"Sure, I will do it now. Those are some signs of pregnancy, but they are also signs of something else too."

The doctor starts the test. I accompany Taylor for the sole purpose of seeing the test. I got up. I walked outside. I couldn't watch it. I went into the hallway. I was walking up and down. Waiting for Taylor to come through the door with the answer. Every sound I heard caused me to jump. My knees were weak. I could not stand it anymore, so I sat on the ground in the passageway. I closed my eyes. Nothing was important to me anymore.

After thirty minutes, the door opened. Taylor walked out with a bright smile on her face. She looked in my direction and hugged her belly with both hands. I screamed in tears. I got up and rushed to Taylor. My knees were still giving way. I couldn't believe what I heard. Like a pet, I dropped to her feet. I grabbed both feet and pulled her closer to me with my ears resting on her belly. I was feeling for the baby. I was listening for something. Taylor was rubbing my head trying to comfort me. She was elated. She whispered while the tears were flowing.

"You were right, honey. You were right. I am six weeks pregnant. We are pregnant. We are going to have a baby."

I do not know where I generate the extra strength, but I had power. The extra strength allows me to lift Taylor into the air. Walking around with her is like a trophy. I did not want to put her down.

"Thank you. I love you more than life itself. This is a miracle. You have a part of me inside you. We will be great parents."

The doctor was trying to console us, but that was useless. We always wanted to start a family. The doctor provides us with guidance on how we will cope during this journey. As we left, I was walking with a purpose. Establishing a shield around Taylor while beefing up security.

The next six months were interesting. Taylor moves from agile to fragile. I was there for her every day. Fixing her hair, tying her shoelaces, and helping her around. Nothing was too small or large for me. She needed to be healthy. I do everything around the house. Taylor stressed that it was important that she remains active. But I was cautious.

We were at home at about seven p.m. that Thursday evening. Taylor was feeling minor pain. She was experiencing some cramps. I was massaging her belly and rubbing her feet. Suddenly she screamed.

"Take me to the hospital. My water broke. Take me now. I feel like I am going into labor."

I have been practicing for this day for six months now. It was important to remain calm. I helped her to the car and rushed her to the hospital. The doctor was notified, and he met us at the hospital. As soon as we reached her, the doctors and nurses started to prepare her for delivery. I need to be strong. The nurse handed me a gown and a mask. It was my wish to witness the birth of my child. Ten minutes into the medical procedure, I heard the baby cry. Taylor was squeezing my hands. It was painful, but I managed. It was a beautiful baby boy. He looked just like me. The baby has Taylor's eyes.

The nurse handed the baby to me. I held my son. He was tiny and handsome. Taylor was resting. Her eyes were gleeful with joy. My work just started. I will keep my son company until Taylor wakes up. He was looking at her. There was no doubt that he recognized me. His eyes are all over the room as if he was searching for his mother. We will be at the hospital until tomorrow. I am going nowhere. I am taking care of my family.

CHAPTER 37

The addition to the family brings us closer together. How close can we get? This is a partnership. The baby's room was painted blue and had several paintings of Mickey Mouse. Conner was attached to us. It was difficult for Taylor to leave him to return to work. The first morning was hard. Being around the baby for four months develops a level of dependency. Taylor gets frustrated when the baby cries and celebrates when the baby laughs. We could not put him down. We worked on shift. When Taylor needed a break, I took over.

It was early Monday morning, and the babysitter was early. She took Conner and was feeding him. We got ready and were about to leave for work. Taylor was turning in every room looking for different things. After thirty minutes, I realized that something was wrong. Every time Conner made a sound, she would run to his rescue.

"Dan, I am not sure of this arrangement. I don't know if I can trust the babysitter to take care of Conner. He is not familiar with her and might cry all day."

I realize that I have a problem. I must convince my wife that the baby will be fine. Understanding the nature of relationships and love will encourage her to allow the child to grow.

"Conner will be fine. Babies have a great instinct that allows them to gravitate to other people. This is a part of their growth and development."

Taylor looks worried. Her eyes were fixated on the baby's

room. As she processed my message, she walked toward the door. I opened the door and let her out. Before I could close it, Taylor was bracing the door with her hands.

"I didn't get to say goodbye. I want my child to know that I will not be here today. He might grow up to hate me if he thought that I abandoned him."

"Make it quick. We are going to be late."

I beckoned the babysitter to bring the baby downstairs. Taylor walked over to Conner and held his tiny hands. Explaining every decision that was taken, and every action that she will take today. Conner was staring at her, fascinated with the ID that was hanging from her shirt. His movements convince Taylor that he understands every word that she utters.

"I want you to be on your best behavior today. Mommy will be back soon. I need to go to work today, but I promise that I will call and check up on you."

Taylor started walking toward the door again. Holding on to the baby's fingers. The sitter followed her through the door. Finally, she let go. The bond was broken. I was able to get her to leave. I understand the bond that a mother has with her child.

As the months went by, Taylor's understanding of the child's development grew stronger. Our love for each other and Conner was unconditional. Every day was a new adventure. Adventures bind the family and force us to love each other more. We were afraid that the existence of Conner might reduce the time that we spent together. We were wrong. The partnership gets stronger. We believe that it was important for Conner to grow up in a loving home. That was easy to achieve. I cannot wait to come home to my family whenever I am away. Taylor's voice became a part of my ears.

My first business trip to California was a test. I was away

from my family for one week. The distance might be far, but we communicate every hour of the day. Taylor was not concerned that my ex-wife was from the state. We develop a level of trust. Love is a beautiful thing. It forces people who are believers in this theory to depend on each other for support. I am blessed to have a loving family. To see the sun shine on me during the rain. Overcoming all obstacles because we work together as a unit. Supporting each other because we are governed by a common bond.

Our parents are the bedrock of our existence. They are a part of Conner's life, and we visit them often. He knows his grandparents and looks up to them for love and support. I used to hate dreaming. It always scares me when I am alone because my mind tends to wander. Taylor causes my life to have a different meaning. The more I think about her, the more I love her. The longer I stay away from her, the more I want to see her.

Taylor thought that love had a ceiling. The road is long, but it has an end. She proves to me that love is infinite. The longer we are together, the stronger our relationship gets, and the more we love each other. Her beauty never fades. I looked at her every day and saw the same person. I understand that she might get older with age. I am blinded by love. Taylor is prettier by the minute.

Every week we go out on dates as if we had just met. The creases of our fingers form to match the shapes of each other. Observers believe that they are glued together. I never feel like letting her go. Even if I forget to hold her, she brings my memory in the line. There are no restaurants, parks, theaters, or ballrooms that did not feel the effect of our love. I am never too busy for Taylor because she is the reason why I am busy. We are more playful than the day we met.

Conner will start middle school soon. We decided to take a Trip to North Carolina. Our houses and parents are still there.

"Babes, we need to split the one-week trip among both parents. Three days each and one day for us. This will allow us to see all our friends."

"Mom is eager to show Conner around. She is no longer interested in me. She believes that I am grown, and she likes younger people."

"I will not interfere with you and your mother. You need to convince her that you were before Conner."

As we reached my mother's house, she rushed outside to meet us. It brings back memories of my youth. Seeing where I was born helps me to appreciate what I became. I am thirty-five and still crave my mother's love. Sometimes I feel jealous seeing the two most important women in my life embracing Conner more than me. Sometimes I feel like a child again. However, that might deprive me of my love and affection for Taylor. I cannot have it all, but sometimes loves tend to conflict with each other.

My mother hugged and kissed us. She knew what I was thinking. Maybe Taylor said something to her. My mother gave me my fair share of attention. I am not selfish. It is Conner's turn.

"Come, my grandbaby, I have a lot of things to talk about. We have gifts inside for you. You do not have to go back to New York if you don't want to."

"Mom, you can have him any holiday if you want," I joked. "We might have another one and replace him."

"Stop playing Dan."

Taylor gave me a friendly smack on my hands. It was joyous to be back in North Carolina. We are creating memories. Memories that will last for a lifetime. I hugged Taylor from behind. Reprimanding the hand that smacked me. I saw the look on my parents' faces. They were pleased that after several years our love had not faded. Their efforts have not gone in vain. The seeds were sown on our love, and they grow into large trees. The trees have blossomed and bear fruits. Sweet fruits capture the eyes.

We left Conner with his grandparents and went to visit Tyler and Brandon. It was like old times. The difference is that I am not alone. I do not go anywhere by myself any more. Taylor is my other half. Together we make one. It was like a party. Tyler was married. I thanked him for helping me in times of need. I am a believer in love, but he was the living testament. Seeing them together gave me hope. Hope that love was real. It is out there, and I was determined to find it. Brandon had a friend with him. He is who he is. He believes that relationships happen by chance and if people were meant to be, it will happen. That is farthest from the truth. Every decision has consequences. The more effort that I put into loving Taylor, it multiplies tenfold.

Life is full of surprises. Some events we can control, and some are left to the creator. We reminisce about past times. Emphasizes the journey that we have in our relationships and the techniques we use to improve them. For me, my journey was long and hard. I started at eighteen years old and was committed for seven years. This relationship caused my first heartbreak. I was devastated. I did not give up. My family and close friends helped me through my depression. Again, the dark side of life found me. I have no energy to focus on the past because Taylor showed me the meaning of love. I am not afraid to show my affection to her. As we talked, our love was on display. Taylor appreciates the way I talk about her. She pulled me closer and showed the world her feelings.

The mountain can never be too high to dissuade me from

climbing it. The road might be narrow, but I will stay on the course. For some people, tomorrow might be another day. For us, it is a special day. A day that we cherish. A moment that demands our attention. As time goes by, our love grows like a giant. The giant creates a protective layer and allows us to live in a safe space.

"All my life, Brandon taught me about relationships. I listened to him and formed my own opinion. His approach might be different from mine. I am not here to judge him. Love requires a diversity of views. I am a better person today because of him and Tyler," I explained.

"I want to be like you one day when I grow up. It might be soon; it might never be. I am floating with the wind. But I would be lying if I said I am not envious of your relationship. I can see the genuine affection that you display for each other. Talking about each other like nothing else around you matters. You softened my heart. Feelings of love that I thought would never cross my mind, are now lingering in my subconsciousness," Brandon confessed.

I looked at Brandon and could see the curiosity in his eyes. He has a genuine fear of commitment, and I could hear the seriousness in his voice. I found a special woman that makes it easy to love her. We did not dwell on immaterial things that did not add value to our life. The past is important to be used as a guide for the future. However, the future is what matters. The future shapes my existence. It bound me to the love that Taylor gives every day.

"I hear so much about you, Brandon. Everybody has their style. Your expressions of love and admiration for Dan and Taylor give me hope. I was molded in love from birth. But the selfishness of my upbringing is nothing if it has no impact on my surroundings. I am sure that in a few months Dan will advise me that he is coming to your wedding," Tyler predicted.

"I am glad that you guys have faith in me when I doubted myself. There is hope for me after all," Brandon joked.

This is a history lesson. A history lesson about love. Love is not formed in a vacuum or bought on the street. It is achieved from the effort and affection that Taylor and I placed in ourselves. In the beginning, I thought that love was a difficult subject. It is not. Infatuation is a complex subject because it confuses me with material things. A woman with a kind heart who was willing to shower me with material things win my heart. I learn the hard way. I was looking for love and companionship, but I settled for gifts. I was miserable. I could not breathe. It was not too late for me. I will never give up. I changed course because I was determined to find love. In the process, I discovered that love was before me all along.

Last week was a special chapter in our life. Our love was on display in North Carolina among all the friends and families that we cared for. It withstood the test of time. Taylor never leaves my side. We were equal partners in crime. Spearheading the crusade against hate because our effort is worth it. There is a fun game that we play at home. Interviewing each other about love to test the pulse of our relationship. Tonight, we put Conner to bed and explored our love theory.

"Dan, tell me something about me that you do not like. Something that needs changing or improvements."

This was the hardest topic that I got to explore. Taylor has the sweetest personality and the best character of a woman. Most men complain that their wives change the way they dress for bed after a certain age. I giggle every time I hear that comment. I asked Taylor to tone down because my eyes are unable to focus.

After thinking for twenty minutes, I try to come up with something that might start a conversation.

"Stop being so nice. Sometimes I need something to complain about. Every time I look at you, it tempts me to hold you closer."

Taylor's smile was evident. She gets me good, cornering me in a box. I could not get out. After several years together, I could not find one thing about Taylor that needs to change.

"Are you saying that I am perfect?"

"Yes, you are perfect. In my eyes, you are flawless. I cannot find anything about you that bothers me. In the eyes of others, you are human. In my eyes, you are an angel. An angel with supernatural powers. Your wings might not be evident, but the things that you accomplished can only be explained by God."

Taylor shuffled across the bed and into my arms. Placing her forehead on mine and whispered in my ear.

"Thank you for being there for me. People might say that love is blind, and that God does not put people together. We prove them wrong. It was the work of God that brought us together. Our collective effort molds the love that keeps us relevant. There has never been a dull moment in our life. My feelings are stronger for you every minute of the day."

Her eyes were blinking faster. Her lashes were touching mine. I am still shy. I close my eyes and imagine what is going to happen. The clock is ticking. Taylor's breath is massaging my face. She is looking right through me. I open my eyes. The most beautiful lips staring down mine. Admiring her facial structures from inches away. I could catch the words coming from her mouth. Love is a strange thing. It is real. It enables me to understand love in all forms. I want to kiss her. She knows what she is doing. My lips are trembling, eager to express themselves. Not through words, but actions. Taylor was playing a game. She was tormenting me. I am vulnerable. Taylor is enjoying it. I realize that love forms a union. A union that makes us one. We have the same breath, the same heart, and an appetite for each other.

"I love you with all my heart. You are the woman of my desire."

As I say that, Taylor moves away. I thought I did something wrong. But the night has just started.

"I am going to make tonight special for you. The gift of love was given to us. We have the power to make it better."

Taylor climbs off the bed and heads into the bathroom. My mind was wandering. She took a bath an hour ago. Surprising is a good thing. Anything from Taylor is worth waiting for. Should I close my eyes? I want to see what happens. The suspense is killing me. I reach for the bottle of water on the night table. I drank half of it, and I still feel thirsty. The light in the room was off, but the moon was out. It was shining through the window and providing sufficient light for the room. I could count the stars. They were forming a pattern. I saw that pattern in my dream. The galaxy was in the shape of a heart. There were two galaxies. The stars in each galaxy were moving. In minutes, both hearts form one. This is a sign. Suddenly Taylor emerges from the bathroom. She was clad in a beautiful red dress. Her entire body structure was evident through the dress. The length of the dress was just below her waist. She walked over to me and held my hands. I climbed off the bed and stood to the side of the bed. I was looking at her. I did not blink. I did not want to miss anything.

"Do you recognize me?" Taylor whispered.

She is the sexist angel in heaven. I was looking for her wings. Why did she ask me if I recognize her? She has been my wife for six years. The more I admire her, the more I want her. The more I stared at her, the more I started getting flashes. Taylor looks like the woman in the red dress in my dream. I start to think. I remember the woman who appeared in my dream when I was having marital problems. Her questions were on my lips. She wants to know if I love Casey. It is getting clearer now. How could that be me? It was Taylor all along that was revealing herself to me. She is my guardian angel warning me of the danger around. I should have listened to the voices in my head. She was very clear.

I drew Taylor closer to me. My eyes were fixated on her. The feeling of our first night together reappeared. I was sweating. I was trembling. My knees were weak. I kissed her passionately. Her lips were soft. I did not want to stop. The stars are looking in from the outside. They were jumping up and down. Celebrating that moment with the angel before me. It was simple. This is what love is. My love for Taylor is so strong that she remains the figment of my imagination. They form the visions I had several times in the past. The angel was a gentle soul. Teaching me the meaning of love. If I doubted life and the happiness that it brings, that doubt would disappear. I am thankful to Taylor for showing me what true love is. We understand each other and keep each other company even in our sleep. I remember the nights and the lonely nights. I remember the heartbreaks and the depression. But all that memory quickly fades. My mind is occupied with fresh memories. Memories of real love. Memories of lasting friendship. A friendship that I cherish. I have no doubt or hesitation. My life will change forever because Taylor is in my arms. Love makes this possible. Love is not guaranteed, but our love is everlasting.

THE END